GURUJI

II Om Ganpatey Namah II

Dedicated to all the worldwide devotees of
Lord Hanumanji,
The god of Power, Strength and Intellect.

GURUJI

(The Mentor)

SUNIL GOVIND

PARTRIDGE

A Penguin Random House Company

Print information available on the last page.

To order additional copies of this book, contact
Partridge India
000 800 10062 62
orders.india@partridgepublishing.com

www.partridgepublishing.com/india

FROM THE HEART
OF AUTHOR.......

My father late Shri Govindrao Nawkarkar was called as Tatyaji in the entire family. He was very fond of reading and also writing religious literature. In his spare time he used to write *Bhajans* – that are religious poems and some short stories as well. But unfortunately his work remained unpublished and his thoughts could not reach out to the masses. I was impressed by my beloved father's work and inspired by his thoughts. I think the 'Guruji' came out of my pen as inspirations from my father, Tatyaji. I am sure; publication of 'Guruji' will be true homage to him.

While struggling hard to survive in life, a common man has to face many difficulties being surrounded by sorrow and grief. He always finds himself in the thorns of confusions and mystery of misfortune. When fortune does not favor you, it plays cruel role in your life. You cannot run away either from the situation or from life. It is tragedy of common man's life that he finds no clue or solutions to his problems. Nobody, from society, relatives or friends come forward to help him; to support him. Actually, if it happens that anybody comes forward to back him and plays the role of real mentor by giving him proper guidance he might have stood with full strength against misfortune. And know this is the situation when somebody should guide you, to stand behind you to walk on this critical path.

The 'Guruji' is an easy and simple form of literature for commoner to help walk on the path of spirituality with strength and support to succeed against misfortune and drag favor out of destiny too. With the blessings of Lord Hanumanta, I am sure the 'Guruji' will definitely stand behind everybody as a mentor, as a guide and as a supporter.

Respected Shri Morari Bapu always mentions every time that he doesn't have any disciple. Still, I see him at the sacred and highest place of my mentor. Without the blessings of mentor this endeavor might not have been completed. I am very grateful to respected Morari Bapu.

I am very much thankful to Mr. Jayant Dasgupta of Landmark, India whose inspirations have compelled me to convert this writing in the form of book. I would also like to express my wholehearted thanks to my wife Mrs. Ratna who was curious every day to know what I've written. She pushed me to write every day. My daughter Ms. Prachi and son Rishabh are always there to help and extend wholehearted enthusiastic support to my work. Thanks to both. All the friends and well-wishers were the part and parcel of the whole work. Without their continuous efforts nothing could have been materialized. My salute to everyone.

The publisher M/s. Partridge India and their team that have given artistic shape to this sculpture. I am grateful to all.

Lastly, I am grateful to all of you readers who accepted, admired and loved 'Guruji' so much.

sunil govind.

PREFACE

In today's world nobody is found to be reliable. Even in the religious and sacred field of worshipping–God-devotion we experience fraud activities of saints and sadhus. Beliefs are found to be corrupted. The ancient spiritual science is found to be trapped within the doubtful atmosphere. It is difficult for a common man to go to the bottom of fact and find out the truth. One can't spare time to go in to the details and that's why he keeps himself isolated from the subject. Some of the fraud saints have commercialized the very purpose of worship and devotion. At this juncture when I emphasize and talk about Mentor and its sacred importance, I feel, those are not matching to the present situation.

Still while talking about true mentor (The Guruji), I would say that one may get a true mentor by fortune or by the grace of God. I think it is the Almighty that decide the time, the place and about his meeting. It is so said that it is difficult to identify and recognize true mentor. See, when one would get the intuition by his own intellectual to identify true or fraud that might have been too late. As it has been said earlier, we get good parents by God's bless and alike true mentor too.

In the present practical world we still find some unselfish persons are working for betterment of common man. They are working hard for the welfare of downtrodden people. These persons are devoted to enrich the human life with happiness, peace and prosperity and they think that was the noble service to God in real sense. Only because of these selfless people, ancient cultures still exist in the society by keeping pace with modern culture. This is certainly the power of ancient culture that we can adapt and adjust our-self to modern thoughts with preserving our ancient values and virtues.

In the present story one simple person with least desire for publicity has enlightened the life of depressed women. While working hard in the society for innovative work of building human character, he was never found to be indulged in making propaganda of his devotion, his good deeds, etc. While imbibing values like love, belief, compassion and morality in common man he forcefully restricted misbelief about religion in the mass. In his opinion true religion was the serving to the human being. Without observing any so called traditional formalities the depressed women accepts him as a mentor (the Guruji). The Guruji's simple but effective teachings impress her and her life changes totally.

Her whole life was full of hardships. As it is always being said that 'hard-work is a gateway to successes'. But in the present case the woman had never experienced success to her work in her life. She always worked harder and harder to attain her goals. She goes into a depression, shunning any idea of happiness. But, at some point in her life journey she realizes, to experience the best time in their lives, one has to have a good balance of good deeds. Guruji taught her to walk on spiritual path. Guruji claims that the path he was showing for self-improvement would surely lead towards holistic happiness.

According to your perseverance, your ability and hard-work it may require some time to attain success which may vary from person to person but it is guaranteed to achieve the desired goal and you'll get the treasure of happiness. The way the drunkard walks down on the path and his search ends at a bar, in the same way when a devotee walks on the sacred path of spirituality, the path ends at divine place of worship and God.

Sometimes, miraculously, divine things happen in life and divinity itself comes forward to deliver best for us. It is just searching for us to bring good-luck in our life. After completion over half of the life period the women's life has been enlightened by the mentor (the guruji).

We, for an entire life remain in dilemma and confusion about the existence of God. His existence has always been a matter of discussions, but don't forget! His almighty is always keeping His eyes on us. In day-to-day life when we are struggling, we cannot spare time to pray to God and without expecting any miracles we continue to perform our duties for society, for family, etc. Watching your deeds-your hardships, His almighty is always there to take care of yourselves. He deputes a prophet for your welfare, for your happiness, for your self-empowerment and peace. This prophet is always there to back you and support you to walk on the path of progress. What you need is to identify him, rely on him, follow him and to continue with nonstop efforts to achieve goal. It requires your acceptance and devotion. You can see now all the hurdles of your life are going to be vanished. You need not turn back, on the path of holistic progress. This is true!

The same episode is described here for a depressed woman. The mentor (Guruji) has guided to walk her on spiritual path by introducing recital of *Hanuman Chalisa*.

PROPHET'S ARRIVAL

The train had already picked up speed. On boarding one had to walk through at least two to three compartments to locate a suitable seat. The long distance passengers spread themselves across their berths as if they had purchased the berths and were the owners. For heaven's sake, we were monthly pass holders too! We have to travel only for an hour by sitting. We too had the railway permit to travel by this superfast train. By the time I found a seat the train was in good speed. And now, a full hour's journey by this superfast train! The seat next to me was vacant. A gentleman, who had followed me in, took the same seat, a little away from me. I had seen him quite a few times in the town but didn't know him personally; nor did I know who he was. And from his conversation with me that followed, it was obvious that he too did not know me. He had a dark but lively countenance with expressive eyes. Well-built, with wavy hair and a cheerful face, he looked as if he was just out of bath. His attention was drawn towards the ring on my ring finger and he said, "You have worn the ring on the wrong finger."

I stared at him in suspicion. We hardly knew each other; how could he pass such a personal comment? In the course of my daily train travel I had come across many such chatty males trying to get talking with good looking women for no reason in particular. I glanced at him. He appeared elegant and from a cultured background. The sobriety, the gentleness, the refinement certainly enhanced his demeanour. That he was a perfect gentleman was apparent from the serenity in his expression, the mystical sparkle of his eyes, clean teeth and his overall body language. I realised that the words had been uttered simply and innocently.

Right from the beginning I was biased towards well-dressed men and women. It was my belief that people who took care of their grooming must also be leading a good life. I had the habit of minutely observing people -the way they act, their body language, etc. and based on these I tried to assess their character. This had become a hobby with me for quite a while now. And going by my standards of personality assessment I found this person to be a thorough gentleman.

So I said, 'An astrologer had advised me and so I'm wearing it on this finger. Are you knowing of anything on the subject?'

'Yes, a little', he replied. 'This should have been worn on the little finger.'

I said, 'But how can you make the statement so confidently? You don't know anything about what I have gone through in life. I narrated my problems to a good astrologer and on examining my horoscope he advised me to wear this particular stone in the ring".

He replied quietly, 'Look, I don't know you; nor do I have any ulterior motive in making this statement. It's only that I couldn't bear to see this and so I made the comment. I'm Sorry.'

I was totally perplexed by his words. Seriously…. especially since I hardly knew him!

During the train travel it is usual to find chaos of vendors. It's just like a small market on wheel of Cold drinks, Cigarettes, Tea, fruits, etc. Routine train travel has become common over the last few years. Officers, employees, teachers, etc. and the others in service staying around hundred kilometres from their places of work commute to and fro daily and manage their jobs. They use state transport buses, trains or whatever other mode of transport is available at their disposal from the city or the district. This kind of commuting is commonly referred as up and down travel. If the train or bus travel takes up to one to two hours, then it is feasible to travel up and down. The office timings are from ten o'clock in the morning and one is expected to wind up by five thirty, in the evening. In order to reach office by ten o'clock, those living in the city have to leave by seven to seven thirty, in the morning by train or by bus so as to reach office in time. In the evening at the close of working hours one has to catch either a train or a bus and reach home by around eight o'clock in the evening. This is the routine life for the working class commuting daily to and fro to make a living. Travelling is an irksome exercise for daily commuters. At times the train or bus is very crowded and one has to travel standing all the way for a couple of hours. At times it is the same story on the way back. So they reach office exhausted and return home exhausted. This is a routine matter, but there is no way out. The family is stationed in the city and the children's schools-colleges; medical care, shopping, etc. are all set there. And it is neither possible nor affordable to shift some eighty or hundred kilometres away from the settled place.

In fact earlier as there were fewer options available for travelling, employees, officers and the teaching fraternity, whenever they got a transfer order, took their families along and settled in the place of transfer. Although this disturbed their living pattern, they had no option but to move to the new place as they could not do without their jobs.

Now the government has introduced bus services connecting every village to the cities. It has become possible to travel from any village to any city and vice versa, at any time of the day. Trains too have been introduced on a number of routes. Moreover, as train travel is much cheaper, it becomes the most affordable mode of travel especially for those commuting to and fro on a daily basis.

Sometime later, I noticed, this gentleman has seen temple outside the window of running train and for a moment, he wished by touching his hands to his head with closed eyes.

Breaking the silence between us I casually remarked, 'Sir, Do you believe in worshipping idol?'

He said yes he believed. Idols were nothing but the symbols to be worshipped and this could lead us on the way of spirituality. Before going in to meditation Guru or sages give a very simple process to make entry in the world of spirituality. Different modes of worships are taught by ancient scriptures. We can say; Life is divine worship. The entire (*puja*) worship system and sacredness of worship that are described in the Hindu scriptures, are found scientifically accurate and very useful to live happy life. There is generally criticism over worshipping an idol. But nothing is wrong in worshipping an idol in the beginning. Idol-worship is only the beginning of religion. There can be different stages of worship. The first one is the worship of idols. The idol

_____

Puja – Worshipping God

is symbolic. Symbol is definitely helpful for beginners at initial stage. In std. first, one can start learning with the help of symbols only. Hindus very well know the images, portraits of deities and so many symbols. In the same way, crosses too! Those symbols are necessary for beginners for developing concentration. Keeping in the mind the symbols, one can start worshipping. This can be his first step to walk on long spiritual journey. These symbols are not compulsory for every worshipper. Even these are not required to yogis or sages. Though the beginner worships the idol, he has to feel 'His' presence in his heart. His mental eye remains spotted towards the Lord. One has to superimpose God and His attributes on the idol. This way the worshipper starts to feel the existence of lord in the idol. He begins to feel his presence everywhere. Hindu scriptures, which initially guide for idol-worship later on described the theory of meditation. The aspirant then is taken, step by step, to higher stages of meditation through the worship of the idol. Another way to take aspirant on spiritual path is chanting of sacred mantras. The mantra is whispered as it is meant to be kept secret and is chanted internally or externally by the mediator. The power of the mantra lies in the proper utterance of its sacred sound. Mantras chanting are also help concentrate within inner self by not allowing a single waste thought within your mind. Regular chanting of mantras help purify your thoughts and charge the subtle spiritual energy within you. Keep internal worship in your heart to remain consistent. You will attain completeness. The technique of repetition of mantras is called as *Japa* meditation. *A* mantra is chanted aloud or internally continuous repeating makes awareness stronger and helps centralized concentration. To count down the numbers of mantras chanted, beads of a rosary are turned. Generally, rosary contains one hundred and eight beads and the mantra is chanted once for each bead.

Further, there is *Dhyana* meditation supported with *pranayama*. The intention behind worshipping or meditation is to develop a spiritual awareness in our life.

Every aspirant according to his strength or devotion makes efforts to realise the Infinite. By gathering deep and deep spiritual knowledge he himself merges in the supreme power and attains the goal. The priests or Gurus are like kind mothers. By following their directions the aspirant can go ahead on the spiritual path. ....

Till the journey of about one hour finishes, I could benefited by this divine discourse. Thank God. I felt very much blessed today by meeting enlightened personality. I found in him a hidden spiritual person and he elaborated the subject further in detail. This train journey was just like a sacred discourse by an enlightened personality.

I listened to my inner voice whispering to me. This was no ordinary person. I felt a sparkling, divine aura around him. Perhaps God had sent his messenger personified in this form to guide me. Unawares I had a feeling that this person was definitely endowed with some kind of supernatural powers that would help me in improving my life; open up a new perspective of looking at life.

I remember somewhere I had read about prophet. According to Christianity prophet is a man who speaks

---

Dhyana – Contemplation, concentration & Meditation.

Pranayam – Systematic & regulated breathing system prescribed by Ancient Yoga & Spiritual Teacher Patanjali.

on behalf of God. Prophet is 'His' messenger. A prophet receives the Lord's word for betterment of mankind. A prophet, then, is the authorized representative of the Lord. It is said that Scriptures are the words written by the prophet. God speaks through him. A prophet is a teacher.

A prophet, then, is the authorized representative of the Lord. While the world may not recognize him, the important thing is that God speaks through him. He receives revelations from the Lord. These may be new truths or explanations of truths already received

Through 'His' prophets, God reveals 'His' will to the entire world. Sometimes, for our safety and help, a prophet is inspired by God to prophesy about future events. The prophet is the only person who receives revelation from God and will never teach anything contrary to the will of the Lord.

Within seconds I was convinced that this was the person deputed by God for the sake of building my future whose influence would instil positivity in my life by removing the sorrow eclipsing my life. This was arrival of a prophet in my life. And unawares, my face softened into a smile. For once I was in a cheerful mood during my journey.

THE IMPRESSIONS (SANSKARAS)

I was born in a tribal family. My childhood was spent there and I also did my primary schooling from that region. Hence I was strongly under the influence of tribal and nomadic culture. My father, a Government Officer was a highly corrupt individual. In India, we can see some people while working in government departments are notorious for making money through unfair means. They indulge in innumerable ways of harassing people to fill their pockets with easy money. This leads to drinking; squandering money on luxuries, etc. till it becomes a way of life with them. And they start believing this to be a status symbol. When I was Growing up, I got very good grades in school. I was a much disciplined student. In fact teachers were considering me as 'A' grade student always. When I was a little girl, I never felt really loved. I felt much rejected all the time in my family. My parent always, I found, indulges in conquering over small family issues. These causes were sufficient to lower down my self-esteem. Result, I could not love myself. My mind had truly accepted these abuses.

My mother was unhappy with the state of affairs. She too hailed from a tribal community but her family was a comparatively cultured and well off. She had completed tenth standard in the olden days. Mother was very intelligent and being cultured her-self, wanted her children to grow up with good values. We were two siblings – my elder brother and I. She was always anxious that we should not be influenced by our father's loathsome behaviour.

When we born we born with *sanskaras* the impressions. Our mind evolves through the impressions received through the senses in the womb of mother. We born with hidden embedded *Sanskaras*. Those *sanskara*s are permanently imprinted in the mind.

Your thoughts and nature depend upon the nature of your *Sanskaras*. If you have good sacred pure *Sanskaras* stored, those will be reflected in present thought process; bad *sanskaras* will surely be displayed like wisely. Some thought-waves are raised in the mind due to situations happen around us. This creation of thought waves embedded in subconscious mind. The subconscious mind is otherwise known as the unconscious mind. The location of this subconscious mind is the cerebellum. The thought-waves are preserved in subconscious mind which we call as memory. This memory of the past recollects in the conscious mind which creates certain impression in our mind; this is known as *Sanskara*. Our conscious mind makes all the opinion on the base of data preserved with us in subconscious mind. Even our total behaviour, we can say, is due to the *sanskaras* imprinted on our subconscious mind. A *Sanskara* is formed in the subconscious mind as soon as we go across the event. At any time, this *Sanskara* can generate a memory of the past happenings. All *sanskaras* exist in the mind. We can say our real enemy is embedded hidden evil *sanskaras*! Those directly affect our character.

Thus while my mother's virtuous influence was moulding us children into being good human beings, simultaneously the father's immoral influence contributed towards our utter confusion. Father's behaviour was the cause of the daily squabbles between the parents. At times under the influence of alcohol he would abuse my mother physically, which resulted in my mother being bed-ridden for days on end.

Our values in life are such that they keep influencing us in an on-going process and emerge in our memory from time to time at any challenging juncture in our lives. Like a still burning flame in the mind, they show us how to take on life during difficult times. Our conscious that teaches us to discriminate between good and bad, is the outcome of the collective values inculcated in us over a period of time. That is why it is the duty of the parents to ensure that good values are inculcated in the family. And in turn it becomes our duty to inculcate the same values across the society at large. This is so because values are not a medicine that we can simply make a person gulp down and order him to be cultured.

Our mind involuntarily observes the way our parents, elders, siblings conduct themselves, a kin to a TV or a radio. When we press a button to put on a TV or a radio, it immediately catches the default channel. Similarly our mind observes the happenings in our surroundings and makes a note of it. Conversely, by his behaviour whether at home, in office, or in the outside society, a person influences people around him and thus unknowingly contributes towards creating their value system. This is an unending two way process.

DIVINE BLESSINGS

Here the summer is extremely harsh. In May the temperature rises to somewhere between forty three degrees to forty eight degrees. I remember, It was the sixth of May. That day I was on railway platform waiting for the train. The train was late by about thirty to forty minutes. I saw again that enlightened personality, the prophet, at the station. I was very much delighted to see him to be there. Unaware of my presence on station he was reading some book sitting on the bench. He was also waiting for train arrival. I was very curious to have a talk with him. Why it was, I didn't know; but I was dammed sure that this man is very different and he is not normal human being. He must have some divine power. He must have different aspect towards human life. His valuable thoughts are like god gift and may show a right path to others to live a blissful life. I want to be benefitted in my life by his valuable guidance. So, I did not hesitate to disturb him and talked formally. I requested him to give me time to see him to talk extensively. I wanted to have answers on many more questions in my mind. So, he consented and we decided to meet at Sangam Restaurant. Summer was at it's high and in the heat of 1:30 in the afternoon we met at the decided place.

I told Sir all about myself, about my hard life.

He asked me my name and I replied, 'Kama'.

He kept on looking at me askance, 'Sorry?'

Probably he had heard such a name for the first time.

'What kind of a name is this, 'Kama'', he wondered.

I said, 'Sir, my name is Kamini Naitam. All at home call me by my pet name 'Kama'; so I am Kama.'

'Oh! 'Kama' is pet name! But I will call you Kamini.'

'I too nodded, Hmm…'

After some formal discussions,

Sir said, 'Why don't you go for spirituality?'

'What do you mean by spirituality? I asked.

Sir exclaimed, ' You are a child!! '.

Seriously, I knew nothing about spirituality. The word spirituality was new to me. In this context Sir had called me a child. I was no doubt completely ignorant in this respect and I had frankly admitted it to Sir. His expression held a mixture of a faint surprise and a smile. Such a grown up woman, a lecturer, and hasn't ever heard of spirituality! That must be the essence of his smile.

'Sir, from where do I start?' I asked.

Sir looked around a little bewildered. I sensed that his reaction was similar to that of a swimming coach when a novice asks him, ' Now can I jump in the water?'

Since the subject was so difficult to understand me in a short time, I forcefully requested sir to visit my residence whenever he finds spare time; to discuss to learn spirituality. Sir consented to come.

One fine Sunday morning Sir visited my house. Immediately on his arrival, I offered a glass of drinking water to Sir, since it is customary in India to do so for guest. After some formal discussions Sir started to talk on the subject of spirituality.

Sir said, 'Are you an aesthetic or non-aesthetic (believer or a non-believer)? I am not asking if you believe in God or not. There is something called cosmic energy present in the universe and if you believe in this divine concept.'

'Of course, I am a believer', I said.

Since childhood I had seen my mother following rituals. She would go to the nearby Shiv temple and offer her prayers. I would imitate and follow my mother; light incense sticks and always prays for everything to be fine. Mother had told us that the invisible power, meaning God, was always with us and we should pray to him so that he is always there to protect and guide us. I had read about this even in the scriptures.

Then Sir said, "From tomorrow onwards you start (chanting) reading *Hanuman Chalisa*; daily"

And Sir handed over one small copy of *Hanuman Chalisa* from his valet. I immediately bowed down for blessings. Sir kept his palm on my head touching smoothly. This was the arrival of a prophet in my life as a mentor, the *guruji*! I became the disciple of this enlighten personality without any more formalities. I accepted wholeheartedly as a *Guruji*. Now, he is my *Guruji*.

As soon as *Guruji* kept his hand over my head, I was transformed. I surprisingly had felt superpower vicinity. The touch was miraculous and my spirit merged. It felt like high power electricity flown in to my body. My consciousness, fully alive, was now totally connected to divine power. I knew that everyone and everything is connected to it. I started to realize the power of God. The touch of the *Guruji* signifies the existence of superpower in every human being and always for ever. Only what it needed is a enlighten personality to give you a super touch. Within the touch it was the cure for all diseases; within the touch was the truth of knowledge. Indeed, the touch was wisdom and love beyond all comprehension. The time had come to think whether I would walk on spiritual life or normal life. For a moment I felt that an angel is standing before me and not guruji; asking to walk in the awesome world of holistic happiness without fear of anything.

Guruji in the role of the angel is asking me to forget sadness, poverty, envy, jealousy, worries and tears to walk on spiritual life. This angel said me as to myself be in the safe zone henceforth. You know, one has to work hard and make rigorous *Tapasya* to arrive at this stage too. It was all due to the divine blessings of *Guruji*. Because of Guruji I could attain the present situation which is nearer to enlightenment.

The angle at once asked me several questions, and I answered to them, without hesitations. It was one to one talk. Angle was communicating directly.

His angelic voice asked, 'Have you ever felt this much powerful?'

I answered, 'No.'

'Have you ever felt internally charged this much?'

'No.'

'Have you ever felt this much love?'

'No.'

'Have you ever felt this much completeness?'

'No.'

'Have you ever experienced this much peace?'

'No.'

'have you ever felt this much bold and sound?',

'No'.

Now, my attitude underwent a change. To my surprise, I began to feel a persistent generation of supernatural powers within me like generation of electricity. This time, I realized that my body had developed a strong heart with strong muscles also, to accommodate this much of the power.

Guruji means Guru the mentor. Guru is at equivalent status of God, say the Hindu scriptures. The English word 'guru' has its etymological origin in the *Sanskrit* term and means a "Hindu spiritual teacher or head of religious sect; influential teacher; revered mentor." The guru is a spiritual teacher teaches the disciple to lead on the path of attaining spiritual progress. He enlightens the mind of his disciple. This is the reason why, the guru is considered a respected person with saintly qualities.

Apart from usual spiritual works Guru's sphere of instruction now included subjects like imbibing the values in human beings to make their life full of love, peace, compassion, devotion, satisfaction and humanity.

There were gurus as well as disciples found described in age old Indian scriptures and literary works. Gurus were instrumental in ancient educational system and ancient society. By their creative thinking they brought prosperity to various fields of learning and culture. The most popular story of a young tribal boy Ekalavya on being denied teaching by Dronacharya, decided to build his statue and practised the art of archery. Even he became superior to Arjuna, the master archer, who had learnt the art in presence of the living guru. Later on Eklavya had been asked by Guru to cut and give his thumb as *Gurudakshina* or fees. We will find a great history of the institution of the guru has evolved many spiritual aspects of Indian culture and transmitted spiritual and fundamental knowledge.

HANUMANT DOCTRINE

The *Hanuman Chalisa* is a prayer consisting of forty numbers of stanzas. Prayer is a simple form of yoga. It is strong and proven belief that when we pray to Lord Hanuman with a pure heart and an unshakeable faith, he is sure to come to our rescue - The devotion of Lord Hanuman to Sri Ram is unparalleled.

The *Hanuman Chalisa* was written by the famous 16th century sage, Goswami Tulsidas. In the Ramayana, Hanuman occupies a crucial position. He is the embodiment of auspiciousness, courage, devotion, eloquence, physical prowess and victory. It was only through Him that Sita and Rama could be reunited. Sita represents the Earth, the field, Mother Nature, creativity, abundance. Rama is the spiritual potential, which has been lost from creation. Hanuman represents the forces and teachings that can reunite the creation and spirit. It is through the lessons that we find in His character that the realm of divinity can transpire itself in our society. The *Hanuman Chalisa* was written by Goswami Tulsidas which is significantly contained in itself the entire message of the life and character of Hanuman.

Hanumanji, the well-known monkey god, can be seen in temples throughout India. In some temples his image is found alone standing with a mace in the right hand. In many posters and photographs we find Hanumanji sitting in a devotional posture before Rama and Sita. In the Valmiki Ramayan *[Kishkindha kanda (Chapter), sarga (Verse) 66]*, the story of Hanuman's birth is narrated. According to this story Hanumanji was born to Anjani (her mother). Hanuman's other names are *Hanumanta* and *Pawansuta*. He is also called as *Vayuputra* (the son of *Vayu*-the winds). He is known as the god of power and strength. Hanumanji maintained celibacy through his whole life. Hanumanji's tales valour is found in great detail in the Ramayana along with Rama, Hanuman is invariably worshipped. So many interesting myths are popular and known to every hidus regarding this god. Soon after His birth, Hanumanji expressed his desire to catch the rising sun as He thought it to be some ripe fruit. Hanumanji wanted to put the sun into his mouth. Hanuman was born on the full moon day *(Pournima)* of the Hindu lunar month of *Chaitra*. This day is celebrated as *'Hanuman jayanti'*. That is the birth day of Lord Hanuman. Hanuman is also known as Hanumant.

The scripture Ramayana state that His complexion was yellow and glowing like molten gold. His face was as red as fire. He was very talented with the learning of *Shastras*. He had the mastery over eight types of *siddhi* and all sciences. This God was the ninth author of grammar.

When Rawana kidnapped and abducted SITA, hanumanji had performed important assignment in the search operation. Hanumanji became the greatest and the most faithful associate of Lord Rama. Hanuman's mental

---

Shastra – Science, Law, a monograph
Siddhi – enlightenment, divine illumination

state when He went to search for Sita in Ravan's harem is indicative of his noble character. Seeing beautiful wives of Rawana he could not be overpowered by lust. Many saints acclaimed Hanuman as one having mastery over His senses; literature, philosophy and the art of oratory. Thus his worship recommended and advised strongly in the society.

Hanuman represents energy, skill and devotion. Hanuman is also considered as the promoter of the science of music. Marathi Saint Ramdas had emphasized the worship of Hanuman. Saint Tulsidas established may temples in North India too, and gave importance to worship of Hanuman. Hanumanji is everywhere. He is *pavanputra*; he can move in all directions. The great Indian saint of present time Respected Morari Bapu says 'by *Hanumant jaap*, we can be free from disease and free from all pain. *Hanumant jaap* is very effective for mental sickness and spiritual malice Hanumaji inspires us and gives us peace of mind."

Lastly, Hanumanji is a *pawanputra* means the son of air. Hanuman is present in each breath. We inhale and exhale air which carries oxygen. Without oxygen no one can survive. Hanumant doctrine is the life.

One day a question raised in my mind so I asked

'Guruji, I have a question.'

'What is it? Come out fast", said guruji.

'During my childhood whenever I visited the Hanuman temple, the men and the boys would see the God and pay obeisance. But my mother would never allow me to do that. The other women folk too would offer their prayers from a distance. When asked, my mother told me that women were not supposed to touch the Hanuman idol.'

Guruji agreed; 'that's right and there is a good reason for that'

'What is the reason?' I was curious.

Guruji replied, 'Some women go to the temples even during their periods and destroy the sanctity of the sacred place. And God Hanuman is considered a very aware deity. So this rule has been made merely as a preventive measure, to protect the sanctity of the idol."

I said, 'But guruji, you are asking me to recite the *Hanuman Chalisa*!'

'My dear, reciting does not mean touching.' continued Sir. 'Our Morarji Bapu, whom I consider as my mentor, has so often emphasised in his discourses authentically that women too had a right to recite *Hanuman Chalisa*.'

"Oh, that's correct! Reciting certainly does not amount to touching! " I said.

Guruji, "Yes, after the daily recitations once you have memorised *Hanuman Chalisa*, you can recite it anywhere, anytime, sitting, standing, travelling, at leisure …".

DEPRESSION - A KEY TO SUCCESS

I wasn't so good looking during my days at the middle school. I was an ordinary girl reticent, uncommunicative and completely engrossed in my studies. Continuing conflict between my parents affected the ambience at home and drove me to find solace in my studies. I would immerse myself in my studies and made it my only recreation in life. There was a reason for this. Whenever there was an argument at home, my elder brother would quickly pick up a book and start studying. He was terrified that in the course of their fight they might get at him too. Remembering those times I get a feeling that providence must have showered us with brains because in spite of the state of affairs prevailing at home my brother managed to complete his graduation in medical science. and become a doctor. I too cleared my matriculation with high scores. During the course of time, I had started blossoming. I was entering puberty and was becoming aware of the changes taking place within me. Flattering glances of the people around me made me realise that I was probably the most shapely, tall, attractive personality around the class. My hair was jet black, extending to my waist. The black of my pupils matched the shade of my black hair and were encircled by my natural eyebrows. Eyes were large and expressive. Lecturers in the class couldn't take their eyes off me when teaching in the class. As I excelled in my studies all students as well as the entire junior college faculty looked up to me. Things were no different outside the college. On the road too glances by people convinced me of my uniqueness.

Beauty bestowed on girls is a divine gift. We are not aware of our attractiveness until the admiration in the eyes of onlookers and the comments of our friends make us conscious of it. Even relatives talk about us admiringly to others and that pleases us no end. It is a blissful wave passing through you, like the feeling created in the ambience of a stream of cold water quietly curving its way through the greenery of the mountain!

The neighbourhood aunt would often tell my mother in my presence, 'How pretty you're Kama looks! You will never have any problem marrying her off. She will be picked up in no time.'

On this my mother would say, 'Oh its right! Just be quiet.'

When she said thus, I would quickly run inside and taking the small mirror from the cupboard stand by the window and stare at myself in the twilight. I did not feel anything unusual looking at myself in the mirror. I had been seeing myself for so many years; I looked the same! It is not for us to decide how beautiful we are. What we need is the approval of others.

Eventually I cleared my matriculation. My grades were good and I started planning to go in for medical studies. However, conditions at home denied me the opportunity. My brother was already doing his graduation in medical sciences and therefore the situation at my home compelled me to go for simple graduation.

No sooner had I complete my graduation, my mother had already found a boy for me. My attractive personality and youthful figure were drawing people towards me causes my mother was becoming increasingly anxious. And I felt that was the reason why she worried a lot about my marriage.

An engineer doing business as a building contractor was often a visitor at our home. He told my mother that he was in love with me. His one-sided love and affluent business appealed to my mother. And she immediately consented to our marriage. Lastly, I was engaged to be married. In our times our likes and dislikes, our choice of a partner were not taken into consideration at all. The entire future of the girl was decided solely by the parents.

In fact, marriage is treated as a sacred ceremony in India. It not generally witnessed by Judges. It is witnessed by the fire. The ceremony is to light sacred fire. It is created from *Ghee* (clarified butter) and wooden wicks. *'Agni'* 'the fire god remains the witness to this sacred marriage ceremony. *'Saptapadi'*, also called the 'Seven Steps' are performed before the lightened fire. Amid the chanting the seven blessings seven steps are completed around the fire. By walking around the fire both the bride and grooms are strongly bounded for a lifelong strong union. This is considered the most important part of the ceremony. And this is a traditional process of performing marriage rituals for which every marriage aspirants are waiting for. The bride and groom will make seven encirclements around the sacred lighted fire. Holding hands, they take oath with the seven

---

'Saptapadi' – A ceremony in Hindu marriage system when the newly married couple perform walking seven rounds around the fire

steps. They take oath jointly in the presence of fire for their common journey in marital life.

The seven steps walked with each other are like an oath for your love and friendship with each other. Your promises are witnessed by divine fire as a God's truth and justice. A kind god showers blessings. The couple is blessed with blessings. Parents, relatives, friends and all the members of societies who attend the ceremony bless in several ways. The couple got blessed for inseparable and firm friendship.

May the couple be blessed with happy family life! May this couple be blessed with prosperity and strong bond of friendship within each other! May this couple live in full harmony true to the life values and virtues! May this couple lay there life to make society healthy and this way they try to make world full of peace and progress!

It seems, in my case all the oaths taken were fruitless and the almighty might not have shown its favour towards my marriage. I was so unlucky that the sacred purpose of marriage found totally ruined off by my fate.

So, I was totally against this marriage. I neither liked his looks nor his business of a building contractor. But as the saying goes; 'man proposes and god disposes'. I did not have the guts to refute my mother in the matter of this marriage; in fact, the thought didn't even cross my mind! Abyss!

This is when life turns a new leaf. While for some this important event opens up the gates of paradise, others are pushed into the abyss of hell. And that is what happened to me. In no time I realised that my husband was a drunkard and addicted to luxuries. The family was uncultured and had a humble lifestyle. The husband earned well but whiled away his time in the company of drunkards and gamblers. He was a philanderer too and had illicit relations with loose women. My mother, without sparing a thought for my future, had forced me into a life of hell. My husband would demand physical intimacy under the influence of alcohol. He stank of alcohol and cigars, and flames of canine passion spurted from his bloodshot eyes. This person under the influence of drugs did not have an iota of affection in his eyes. I felt that this was not a man but a wild animal gone mad with passion. And as an Indian wife the responsibility of pacifying his carnal urge lay with me. In India a legally wedded wife considers her husband as God. It is a convention propagated down the ages. Once the marriage vows are taken the wife has to serve her husband as a lifelong commitment; think of him as God and continue the life to drag in a state of utter desperation.

I was not at all happy with my relationship with this man. I continued to wear a mask and create a facade of things being fine. And that is the reason things started deteriorating in my life. Marriage is one of the most important events in one's life.

Physical contact between us had reduced to rape and I was hurt, bitter and angry. I wondered at my capacity to bear the pain deep inside me and considered myself to be a captive of my fate. Living life continually against my will was taking its toll on me and ironically it was my beloved mother who was responsible for all my misfortunes. I kept burying my pain deep inside me. Life appeared totally hopeless and I feared losing my soul in the process.

My status in the family was no better than that of a slave. Sex had become a routine torture with a person given to animal passion, who had no love for me. You know the job of this partnership becomes your own 'personal prison'. My life was a virtual prison in which I had been trapped and forced to go through the most disgusting ordeals. I was beaten up, sexually abused and raped. Every time it happened. I was losing my soul in the process. Many times I just wanted to die when I went to sleep at night with him. I felt so dirty, sleazy. Suicidal thoughts engulfed me when I was finally left alone at night. It was as if I had resigned to this life.

Days and months passed by and one day I discovered that I was pregnant. Any hopes of escaping this prison were now laid to rest, once and for all. I had hitherto kept my sorrow and my shame all to myself. But out of nowhere the anger and hurt in me gave way and I decided to leave this prison with my fortune. I was in complete rebellion of the heart. I decided to rebel … rebel peacefully.

When I was two months pregnant, I started going for routine check-ups at the district hospital. I poured out my entire story to the lady doctor who was sympathetic enough to give me a patient hearing. I even suggested abortion but she was against it and instead advised me to return to my maternal home and relax. This was a god given opportunity for me to escape the present situation. My husband had no choice but to give in to the doctor's advice and allow me to go and take rest at my mother's place. There were tears in my eyes and a deep aching pain in my heart. Thus I left my home, silent and determined never to return in future.

One thing to keep in mind that any situation goes out of control, destroy you. I did not necessarily leave only because I was being abused physically and mentally. I left because, I could not handle the pain of a women within me being treated only a thing of fulfilling wild lust of my husband. So, I ran from this situation; I ran from this house.

My perpetually troubled life and my negative approach to life resulted in driving me into severe depression. In the past two to three years people had become accustomed to seeing me this way. My mother too was no different. Depression!! You can define depression in two types. One is when there is too much anger and fears from long time. The second is when a total dissatisfaction with your life resulting into frustration and depression. I got married and depression entered like a virus in to my life. I was the sufferer of second type of depression which really comes from unsatisfied desires.

I'm thankful to the almighty for giving me depression. If it wasn't there, I could possibly not be successful women. I think depression is the fuel that powers your transformation. If you are depressed, be grateful for your depression. It is an essential component to your transformation and evolution. Don't try to get rid of it, leverage it. Depression is a power required to move you forward in a great way. Depression is your key to success.

Motherhood - a Natures Gift

During my sojourn at my mother's place I delivered a baby son. This was once again a turning point in my life. A new tiny life had stepped into my life. Now I was a mother. All my sorrows had been wiped out of my memory. From the time I arrived at my maternal home till the time of my delivery my mother took the utmost care of me. After all she was my mother. She too had gone through labour. She would keep advising me based on her own experiences. My delivery being normal and there being no complications, the ambience in the house was cheerful. Motherhood is no doubt a priceless gift granted to women by providence. Woman's role as mother is at the heart of the struggle for her soul. It makes her both powerful and vulnerable. Feminists seek the power without accepting the vulnerability. Sentimentality or false sentiment leads them from empathizing with the plight of women with problem pregnancies to removing the reputed cause of the difficulty, the unborn child. The true sentiment of motherhood, which accepts pain and sacrifice for the care of both her and another, succumbs to sentimentality.

One experiences the onset of a completely new life. It's as if a completely new world was unfolding before you. Then entire definition of life has changed. The unbearable labour pains bring about a new perspective to life. In fact I might as well add that right from the first day of pregnancy the mind-set of a woman starts blossoming. Each day appears new. Each day starts with a novel thought, making way for new aspirations. One starts visualising new dreams. There is a feeling of rediscovering life's secrets. Dreams and suspense give rise to expectations tinted with a sense of apprehension.

What if it's a boy; and if it's a girl, then? I think the happiness of motherhood is so pure and unique that whether it is a boy or a girl hardly matters. When a woman becomes pregnant, old emotions arises about her mother resurface- anger, affection, guilt, jealousy, dependence, and the need to be a separate individual. At the same time, especially during her first pregnancy, a woman begins to experience directly what her own mother has gone through to produce her. She gains a new appreciation of what is involved in bearing and raising a child. In some ways, therefore, the expectant mother feels more understanding and tolerant of her mother; in other ways former resentments reawaken. Her mother becomes the model to react against or to copy. The mother-to-be may still feel like a child herself; she may fear being overwhelmed, inadequate, or too immature to have a child.

The woman is engrossed in a strange heavenly world of her own in maternal bliss. Other people and the society at large however occupy themselves discussing the gender of the baby. The news of any pregnancy is likely to be well received with a great happiness by a Hindu family. The birth of a child into the Hindu community is a cause for great celebration. They will be particularly excited if the baby is male. Sons are important in many Hindu rituals. The Hindu child grows up in a religious atmosphere; from birth to marriage, a number of religious ceremonies must be performed for the child. The mother supervises each of these with great care. She considers her household and herself blessed with the arrival of children. The true purpose of marriage is thus fulfilled. Sons are also considered to be a sign of approval and show that a couple are leading spiritually pure and good lives. Hindu babies do not receive a permanent name until naming ceremony known as *Namakarna* that usually takes place within ten days of birth. It is important to make sure that both the temporary birth name and the Hindu name are recorded on the child's clinical records.

TO WALK ALONE. .

Days passed by, and gradually my son, Shyam, was six months old ….and then he was one. During this period I had framed my plans for the future. It was decided about not returning to my in-laws' place, come what may. Since my childhood I was very keen to take up higher studies. Plain graduation was of no satisfaction to me.

I now made up my mind to do my post-graduation. I was not going to give in to any adversities; I was determined to fend for myself. I completed my post-graduation and was a gold medallist. My son was growing up. At four he got into Kindergarten and started his academic education. Though older, he was not yet old enough to be left at home when I ventured out. For a while I took a break from studies and stayed at home to look after him. I would wake him up in morning; give him a bath, put on him uniform and so on. The school uniform was very smart and attractive. I would keep staring at my Shyam till he got in the rickshaw and left. Since the beginning he was a bonny baby and was a darling whose cheeks tempted me to keep pinching them. In our times where was the luxury of uniforms? When parents threw us out, we were in school, and when the last bell rang, we would come home. There were no rickshaws or cycles; even footwear were missing. Ours was not a stray case. Other children too were in the same condition.

With the growing influence of western culture in the world outside, the advent of convents ensured that the education field also fell in line. Although socks, shoes, ties etc. were not compulsory, they were considered as a status symbol. Despite being run by convents, pre-school education up to Standard first had become pricey. Convent education was no longer affordable to the simple and lower income strata of society. All of Shyam's and my expenses were borne by my mother, which was awkward for me.

My inherent pride prompted me to start looking for work. If I get a well-paying job, that would take care of my son's education as well as all my expenses. There was a district junior college close by and I applied there for a casual vacancy. By God's grace I got a call for interview and was selected. Now I started my job as a lecturer in a junior college.

On The way of Spirituality

Now, School examinations were over and after the last exams when our school closed for summer vacation and I went to stay with my mother at our town. They were surprised to see me so unusually happy and peaceful. Mother started commenting on the tremendous change that had come over me.

'Kama dear, shall I ask you something?' Mother asked.

'What is this Mom, why are you staring at me with such wide eyes? Haven't you seen your Kama before?' I said simply and cheerfully, 'Go on, and ask whatever you want to.'

Mother said, 'Kama, this time you are looking so much brighter!'

'What is this, Mom, was I never ever fair.'

'Of course you were. But now there is an added glow to your face. You are speaking so lovingly and peacefully. And you are looking so happy!'

"Kali Ma, please keep the evil spirits away from my daughter," said my mother, waving her arms heavenwards. For a moment I felt that from sky our family goddess Kali

Ma was actually looking down at us and acknowledging my mother's wishes.

I didn't know what to say to her. I was speechless. What could I say to her about spirituality? My mother was educated and religious; but the modern interpretation of spirituality that my Guruji had introduced me to, was by far removed from its ancient, conventional and seemingly superstitious version. It was very practical. Though I had grasped the words used by Guruji, I did not have the capacity to reproduce them exactly and as effectively in front of any one. Nevertheless I was now in a happier state of mind. There was no change in the state of affairs, no change in the problems faced by me, no change in the people surrounding me; but still I had changed. And the credit went to my Guruji. I had changed completely in the past six months.

This all could be possible only because of daily meditation practice. And you will be surprise to know that the first sign that you are becoming religious is that you are becoming cheerful. When a man is in the state of sorrow it is very miserable. Numerous scientific investigations have undoubtedly proved that psychological stress can have disastrous effect on the physical health. Never the less, the knowledge of harmful effects alone does not help us much to lead a life free of worries, stress and tension. In meditation, we keep desire for the grace of divine touch so that our soul may bless with inner peace and bliss. Feelings of happiness & joy are the ultimate goal of meditation.

Finding the truth about oneself is the one of the most challenging explorations. Who am I? This is a process that leads to spiritual empowerment which in turn improves you creative thinking. It creates the emotions of love, peace, harmony in your consciousness and helps in reducing stress, conflicts, hatred and anger. Meditation brings out your intrinsic positive qualities which enable you to develop strength of character and a positive outlook on life. You live every moment in a peaceful manner. You are in a self-observation mode and get an idea of your own true self. Besides creating this awakening, meditation also gives you the strength to understand the spiritual rules and principles that are necessary to create a congenial atmosphere in the consciousness, in the society, and in personal interactions.

What role does meditation play in the field of psychotherapy? In certain psychiatric patients self-motivated relaxation is used for awakening inner consciousness for curing mental problems. Emotions, thoughts, memories, impulses, images, self-concepts are all elements of consciousness. Meditation techniques improve self-awareness and thereby assist in raising the consciousness to a unique level. You are endowed with the astuteness to discern your good and bad traits and this goes a long way in character building.

Like any skill, meditation requires practice to achieve satisfying results. More significantly, there is evidence that a simple means exists, the meditation, which relieves stress and re-establishes mental harmony when practiced regularly. By daily practice you can feel meditation as no longer an effort or a struggle. Meditation is not mere concentration; it is beyond that and it is a supreme state of mind. The goal of meditation is to go beyond the mind and experience our essential nature; which is described as peace, happiness, and bliss. By doing a little meditation every day, it soon becomes a natural and easy habit. Meditation calms mind, brings self-composure, and enables one to concentrate. Meditation means turning your attention away from distracting thoughts and focusing on the present moment. Meditation causes disappearance of addictions, dependencies, self-defeating attitudes, hatred and anger. Meditation can be a part and parcel of the daily routine of everyone. Meditation is the process of remaining in conscious state of mind which improves power of concentration, improves memory and intellectual performance; improves love, compassion within. Meditation brings with a sense of enthusiasm, adventure, peace, power and love. Meditation develops consciousness which is much higher and more powerful than the mind. Meditation teaches you to systematically explore your inner dimensions. Meditation helps overcome neurological disorders.

In the yoga tradition, it is suggested to keep your head, neck, and trunk straight while sitting in a meditative posture *(asana)*. The *Asana* is given importance because the position or the attitude you adopt during meditation, affects the outcome of the meditation exercise. It is important for the body to be balanced and to sit straight so that all the subtle physical energies are unrestricted, then meditation will be more successful. Such posture by regular habit of practicing becomes comfortable to facilitate you to deep perform meditation.

Sit on the floor with a mat or carpet, with your back straight and your eyes closed. Then bring your awareness slowly down through your body. Allow all of the muscles to relax down. Now observe your breath, the rate of breathing will slow down and down with the process of letting go of the tension in your mind. Initially the breath may be irregular, but gradually it will become smooth. Once the

---

Asana – A particular sitting position or posture while performing Yoga

body is relaxed and at peace, bring your awareness to your breath. Meditation upon the breath is a favoured technique because *prana*, the breath, is considered to be the life force which is sacred. Attention is given to inhalation and exhalation. On the in-breath you absorb fresh oxygenated air which represents taking in the purifying energy of the divinity. On the out-breath, you expel carbon dioxide and the impurities of the body. This is a simple process called as *Pranayama*.

Continue to observe your breath without trying to control it. At first the breath may be irregular, but gradually it will become smooth and even, without pauses and jerks. Allow and observe yourself to experience your breathing process and you will learn pranayama by practice. Several thoughts may come across in your mind and you can find yourself in restlessness. However, you have only to attend those thoughts simply without reacting. Beware; reacting to the thoughts may disturb you. Then you can come back observing to the breath. Normally we react to all our thoughts and create confusion. In meditation you will learn what miraculous thing occurs inside without reacting. This awesome experience will start giving you total peace and happiness which further begin to explore who you are. You experience inner peace and contentment, you experience relief and self-perfection and you find a respite from the tumult of your life. You have given yourself an inner vacation.

A clean, little fragrant beautiful room in your own house can be selected for meditation where no disturbance is possible. Meditation has an effect on physical places just as physical places have an effect on people. The atmosphere of a place is created by the activities and thoughts that occur there. It is beneficial to select a place at home that is kept specifically for meditation where you can build up the vibrations and atmosphere. Your meditation space should be kept clean and uncluttered. If possible and affordable, do not sleep in the room meant for meditation. It must be kept holy. Take care that you are entering the room after bathed. You must be cleaned in body and mind. Burn incense regularly and keep some fresh flowers always in to that room and make fragrant atmosphere inside the room. Do not allow the persons to enter it who are not of matching thoughts with you. Basically this is the idea of temples and church. Do not practice the meditation in the case of illness or when mind is very miserable and sorrowful. Twice a day meditation is very beneficial. Early morning and the early evening are the two important periods when your body and mind feel calmness. This helps you to have good quality meditation. Meditation is to control the thoughts, desires, lust and emotion arising within.

Meditation is a method of raising self-completeness leading to self–perfection. Meditation is related to inner consciousness and the awakening of the power within. Meditation restores spiritual self-awareness and power to the human soul. Every soul to a greater or lesser extent is spiritually depleted at this time. Loss of spiritual energy and purity has caused character defects, damage to the moral consciousness and a crisis in values. It is the journey within!!

More and more people are adding some kind of meditation to their daily routine either as an effective antidote to stress, or as a simple method of relaxation. Meditating is deceptively simple. Meditation is an essential part of daily living. Meditation is a joyous enterprise. Meditation help cure the cases of drug-addiction and chronic alcoholism.

Meditation and Pranayama can cure all the psychological complications arise in mind. Very recently, Investigators from the Netherlands and US found that yoga is beneficial in potentially effective therapy for cardiovascular health. Yoga incorporates physical and mental health with reduction in the risk of heart attacks and strokes.

So, it was all happiness due to meditation....because of guruji!! Who taught me to live life with smile... who taught me to overcome loneliness...who taught me to recognise who I am......!

So many years after my birth ....I'm living ... yet to learn simple breathing! Guruji taught me how it is proper breathing. I could not explain this much of happiness to my mother.

There was a heavy downpour throughout the night. I had a good night's sleep. At dawn I wondered if someone had emptied a full tank over us from the skies. It was raining cats and dogs. My deep slumber was slightly disrupted. The rain water was pouring down heavily from the skies. Pulling the blanket over my head I started imagining how vast the space inside the cover was, visualising my own colourful world. While at the outside there was heavy rain, inside was the vast world of a creature on earth! For a while I was occupied with my memories of the past. This was then followed by indulging in dreams for the future. Hitherto my life had been full of hard work and intense sorrow. Now too I continued to work hard. But the mind-set had undergone a drastic change. My life was the same but Guruji had taught me to develop a positive outlook. Yes, what we need is a perspective. Then the same thing can be interpreted as good or bad. Many of you may not be interested in spiritual topics and still have to undergo this process because everybody can be spiritual just as they are emotional, intellectual, aesthetic or non-aesthetic or if they are consciously aware of it or not. Therefore, this experience may arise in the life of someone who meditates and does spiritual practices.

If you are undergoing a spiritual transformation it might feel as if it is happening something unnatural in your inside. Don't fear. It is actually an indication of strength and spiritual and emotional maturity when a person undergoes this spiritual crisis.

References to this process are found in many religions and cultures. Old Bible refers is as the dark night of the soul. In ancient Greece, Egypt, India and other cultures monks and saints guide individuals in this spiritual transformation process and teach to identify inner mysteries, spiritual truths and lot of suspense of spiritual world. It is necessary to encounter a spiritual transformation!

The intention is very clear! It is not me to decide the timings of my awakening. It would be according to divine will and destiny. I had never imagined that life could be so attractive, so happy! Really, life was so beautiful!

'Aaj phir jeeneki tamanna hai'. (Today again I would like to live gracefully!)

Guruji had prepared a time-table for me. If fact he had given me a sort of training on how to manage time during the course of day - right from getting up in the morning to retiring to bed at night. There was time to be made for spirituality at any cost. Forty minutes each in the morning and in the evening were reserved for this. So I would get up at 5:30 am and at around 6:45 am after freshening up, sit for meditation. After forty minutes of meditation I would get ready to leave.

'Nearness to God connotes success while distance from him connotes failure. Devotion, love and compassion connote proximity to God and anger, hatred and cruelty connotes distance from him. This is a simple theory, what I refer to as *'Hanumant theory.'*

I remember when I'd asked Guruji, regarding my failure in (Indian Administrative Examination) examination long back; Guruji' had made this statement: May be there was something lacking in the way you studied or in your efforts. And maybe providence regarded this to be the right for you. After all is said and done, this is destiny! We should continue to do our duty without worrying about success or failure because otherwise we are left with only sorrow. Our hard work never goes waste. What you have studied and the efforts you have put in during preparations for I.A.S. will not go waste just because you have failed. The knowledge you have acquired will certainly come handy sometime or somewhere in your life. Failure after putting in such tremendous amount of work will add value to your experiences. It is a great lesson for the future. At the end of the day material joys and sorrows may be measured on the scale of the success one achieves in exams but they are only temporary. Just as we have created the concept that worship, happiness and compassion signify God while anger, hatred and cruelty signify evil. Similarly happiness and sorrow are concepts too. They are connected straight to the mind. The feeling that brings gratification to the mind is happiness and union with God. And sorrow is the exact antithesis.

EVERYTHING FEELS GLOOMY

Guruji, 'How come I don't feel happy or excited about anything I do? Have I defaulted on prayers and rituals for God? Is this feeling the result of that? I am unable to apply my mind to anything. Even a happy event leaves me restless. I can't even put in words what is happening to me. But I am sure you are capable of understanding what I am going through. Only you can tell me the cause of this and also guide me as to how I should come out of this situation.'

Guruji replied, 'What you say is more or less true. Your assessment that you had perhaps moved away from prayers and rituals, and as for me, departure from spirituality, these reasons are often found to precipitate restlessness. The object of my asking you to offer prayers through the medium of *Hanuman Chalisa* was that this medium or reciting *Hanuman Chalisa* would bring you closer to spirituality. And why it's only *Hanuman Chalisa*? That's because *Hanuman Chalisa* is a supreme incantation that brings about a vivid awareness of the existence of *Hanumanji*.

As the saying *Ashta siddhi nav nidhi ke data* goes, *Hanumanji* himself is considered the pioneer of spirituality and it is because of him that spirituality continues to thrive in today's world. Thus *Hanumanji* is the personified idol of spirituality. After surrendering to *Hanumanji* of such repute and with his blessings when we recite the *Hanuman Chalisa* we gradually merge into the *Hanumant* philosophy and attain spirituality. One good thing that is equally important to note is that on your own you have realised having distanced yourself from the practice of spirituality. And it itself will once again draw you back to it. Your restlessness itself is a proof of how distressed you are on parting ways with spirituality and this distress will again get you back on the path to spirituality.

As we make progress in spirituality, so does our character start taking shape. The six vices - irritation, greed, hatred, anger, envy and fear start disappearing from our system. Initially it may be uncomfortable but over a period of time we will find ourselves being gradually becoming free of such and many other vices. We are no more tormented by these sensations when interacting with others in the society.

Simultaneously we are also required to cope with another parallel front within us. Because whilst we are working on the above mentioned vices during our interactions with the outside world, there is no change when it comes to treating our own selves with hatred, envy, anger and loathing. This is probably the main cause of your distress. You might have been fairly successful in controlling your negative emotions when interacting with others but you may still be harbouring grudge against your own self. You may be loathing yourselves. Perhaps you may even be competing with yourselves. How do I explain? You are finding it difficult to comprehend, and it is equally difficult for me to articulate my words. Nevertheless I will certainly make an effort to clear your doubts. So … what I was saying is that there is a huge difference between what you are and what you want to be. And this disparity between your actual self and the self that you visualise yourself to be, has resulted in your dislike for yourself. Now is it clear?'

I said. 'Guruji, but that's absurd! I can't comprehend the difference between the two me's. Could you please elaborate?'

Guruji answered, 'Okay, I understand. Even explaining is tough for me. But it is necessary to tell you whatever truth I have been able to explore'.

Guruji told a story as an example: A post-graduate working as a clerk. After his post-graduation he had appeared for the Indian Administrative Service (IAS) exam but as fate would have it, he did not clear his IAS. He went into lifelong depression. Over the years he got promoted and reached the level of senior accounts officer. Today while he maintains a good living standard, enjoys a status in society, he still considers himself as a clerk as against an IAS officer. This gives us an idea of the difference between his two selves. He is still not able to optimally enjoy his actual life, the way it is going today. In spite of having all the luxuries at his command the urge to become an IAS officer still remains unfulfilled. Thus his real self is far removed from his ideal self. And this percolates down to his loathing of himself. Which means that although he may have apparently overcome his six vices in the outer world, earned a high status in society, have all worldly luxuries at his disposal, still he is unhappy from within. This is because he has not been able to control and overcome the six negative emotions from his system. Perhaps if he had come to terms with his present situation and decided to let go of what he could not be, he would have found immense happiness.

He continued, 'now, from this example I feel you would have understood the difference between the two conflicting identities of the self'.

I said, 'Yes Guruji, now that it is more or less clear to me, I will be more aware of my drawbacks while reciting *Hanuman Chalisa*.'

Most often when I sit for meditation either the cell phone rings, or someone rings the door-bell; and more often than not, I am preoccupied with various thoughts.

THOUGHTS BECOME GARBAGE

How do thoughts emerge in our minds? Present medical science is into research on this subject in a big way. Perhaps they might even be successful in drawing various inferences. But even the ancient sages in India have been found to have done in-depth research on the origin of thoughts. Thoughts arise from within us. They emerge from the neurological network in the brain. When the original thought emerges from the brain we try to mould it depending on the circumstances that we are in. It is our thoughts that decide our character, our behaviour. And that is how our life unfolds before us. It is our thoughts that give direction to our existence. The negative thoughts crowding our brain make a mess of our lives. Similarly, the positive/idealistic thoughts bring about excellence in our lives. Generally it is the nobility of thoughts that make our lives successful. In fact, successful lives are essentially the outcome of noble thoughts. But remember, too many thoughts are a strain on our energy levels. A sensible person entertains only a few, but useful thoughts while most ordinary people have a myriad thoughts passing through their minds which drive them to a state of utter confusion and disorientation.

Such thoughts are also addressed as waste thoughts. Our energy gets unnecessarily depleted by waste thoughts. Instead we can utilise the same energy for useful or creative thinking and give a proper focus to our lives. For this we should consciously pay attention to our line of thinking. It is necessary to put a timely stop to thoughts that are irrational. Once we start making such an effort our thought process will automatically undergo a change. Our way of thinking will be under control. This restraint will empower us to reject silly thoughts and get adapted only to good thoughts.

'But Guruji', I asked, 'How can I control my thinking process?'

Guruji said, 'Yes, that's tough indeed! But you'll definitely be able to do it with regular practice. For this you will have to adopt some of the practices mentioned in yoga. But hang on; don't get stressed over this. I will tell you some of the simple things discovered by me in yoga. For one, you have already been taught pranayam. In that, study the specific part on how to route oxygen to the brain. So whenever the brain gets crowded with waste thoughts immediately try to concentrate on your breath. You will notice irregularity in your breathing process. Once you master pranayam then you will be able to gain mastery over your thinking process.'

I further asked, 'Guruji, please tell me about negative thoughts.'

Guruji, 'Whatever I have said about waste thoughts applies to negative thoughts too. Waste thoughts include neutral as well as negative thoughts. Unnecessary thoughts that come to us, and which in spite of hours of churning in the brain do not lead us to any definite conclusion, are neutral thoughts. In fact according to psychiatrists at least twenty five to thirty thoughts pass through our brains per minute; then imagine how many thoughts we deal with in twenty four hours! Coming back to negative thoughts – vices like anger, irritation, jealousy, vengefulness, selfishness, laziness, greed are the primary source of negative thoughts. A person with the aforesaid vices invariably creates nothing but negative thoughts. Therefore in order to stop the inflow of negative thoughts it is imperative that we first get rid of these vices and inculcate good qualities. A person with a negative attitude not only leads himself to destruction but is also responsible for creating negativity in the minds of those coming in contact with him. I have already told you the causes of negative flow of thoughts. Thus a person with such negative attitude is incapable of ever becoming happy in life. Hence it is unlikely that he will achieve success in life.

In order to make a success of life it is imperative that we adopt a positive attitude. We need to inculcate qualities like compassion, love, peace, devotion, kindness, honesty, fortitude, tolerance, cooperation and happiness within us. Once we imbibe these in our nature our attitude will become increasingly positive and effective, and will definitely help in making our lives permanently happy, blissful and successful. During meditation we do not realise how we are overcome with thoughts and the mind goes haywire. By the time awareness dawns the stage of trance is already ruined. It's akin to the skid experienced by a car while moving at a constant speed on a smooth road.

And what can I say of the thoughts passing through the mind at that time!

I am sitting in meditation now and how my mind got in to my entire life story; see…...

MY MOTHER'S DEATH

In our early days in the village when someone died, they would call for a band for the funeral. Not the entire band party but just about four to six playing the trumpet and some music players. They would mostly play Mahatma Gandhi's famous tune *'Raghupati raghav rajaram, patitpavan sitaram'*. Rich or poor, the instruments would be the same, and so was the music. The funeral would generally last for one to two hours. The near and dear ones would mourn for the departed soul. Formalities like bathing the body, etc. are Indian rituals. The dead body would be sprayed with perfume, dressed in its favourite outfit, decorated with plenty of roses and taken on its last journey to the crematorium in the full accompaniment of the musical band.

I was shocked at my own weirdness. During the sorrowful occasion, all I felt was an overpowering sense of curiosity. When the entire family was in the depth of sorrow, I would be standing there with an impassive face. I enjoyed listening to the *raghupati raghav* tune being played on the band and in fact feel quite cheerful inside. This terrible occurrence happened to come to my mind one day when I was in meditation.

Death …. Death of a family member is an extremely sorrowful event in one's life. It shakes one from inside out.

As against this, death in general is merely a news item. We are definitely saddened by people dying in the country or in the world at large, for whatever reason. But a family member passing away can be a heart wrenching experience. Moreover if the person is close to us then the sorrow is accompanied by a sense of personal loss. In my childhood I would relish the band and the music played at others' funerals. I would literally enjoy it keeping a straight face. But when the person who loved me, my own mother, passed away, I understood the excruciating sorrow of death. Now I knew the pain. It looked as if my mother was lying peacefully with her eyes closed. My mind was suddenly overcome by calmness; the way we feel when looking at a person's expressionless, still, face when he is sleeping peacefully. My mother's face was so radiant and lively! For a moment it appeared as though she was not dead but had merely gone off to sleep. I felt like driving out the crowd that had gather there and telling them that my mother was alive; stopping the musicians and sending them away. For the first time in my life the tune *'raghupati raghav rajaram'* was bleeding my heart.

My mother had suffered all through life and her sheer hard work had produced two doctors in the family —my elder brother was a medical doctor and I had done my Ph.D. She had given these two of the family for social service.

Moreover, five years ago she had founded a training institute in the rural tribal district in order to facilitate quality education with a view to produce qualified doctors, engineers from this backward province who could offer their services to the society. But her death denied her the opportunity of seeing her dreams fulfilled. The institute was well known for the quality of education it offered and that is how she had earned a reputation and was highly respected as the founder, the director and a prominent woman from the tribal society.

The funeral was attended by the heads of a large number of education institutions within and outside the district, political workers, social workers, etc. We relatives had lost sight of one another in that crowd. Truly, my mother had lived up to the saying, *'Marave pari kirti rupe jagave'*. (meaning:a repute after death also). Her last journey from our home to the crematorium had begun. My eyes were blind with tears. So many respected people came close and offered condolences. At times the sad tears apparently gave way to joy. I had started thinking on the lines that I was lucky to have been born to such an illustrious mother. So many high profile leaders were present with us. Instantaneously I felt very proud of my mother and that felt good. But the very next moment the thought that my mother would never ever speak with me again left a lump in my throat and I gave way to tears. It was 1st of April when God had permanently fooled us by gently taking our mother away from us.

In the evening of 1st April amidst the chants of pundits my brother lit the funeral pyre as per the Hindu rites. Besides our relatives there were many women folk who had accompanied us on her last journey. Earlier, as per the local custom women generally did not attend funeral rites at the crematorium. I too had never been to a crematorium before. However, now at my mother's time there were many women accompanying us and no one took any objection. Was this a sign of modernity taking over orthodoxy in the Indian culture, I wondered. My mother had already ushered the process of creating a literate

---

'Marave pari kirti rupe jagave'. A Marathi language popular saying. (meaning:a repute after death also).

society through her educational institution. Probably this was the reason women were dominant in the crowd. As was the custom, the entire crowd waited until the body had been cremated. In the meantime a condolence meeting was also held. The honourable guests made condolence speeches. They spoke about the achievements of my mother and prayed that she may rest in peace.

Guruji also spoke. 'I pray to God that her soul may rest in peace and may she find a place in heaven',

I still remember his words at that time. After speaking at the condolence meeting Guruji came and stood quietly behind me.

When my mother was undergoing medical treatment at the Hinduja Hospital in Mumbai, Guruji would often come to meet her and cheer her up. During his last visit to Mumbai he could not hide his tears from me. They did not escape her notice either.

On seeing his tears mother said, 'Guruji, you too? What's this? You have always boosted me up. I am what I am only because of you. Guruji, in the last five years you have brought about a complete change in my life. I owe all my success to you. You have made me brave and shown me the way to success. And now how come you are losing hope?'

I started to sob. Guruji controlled me with teary eyes.

Mother continued, 'You cannot lose hope. Now my time is up. Henceforth as her Guruji you will have to be the pillar of support for my daughter.'

Wiping off his tears and pretending to smile Guruji silently gave his consent to offer his support to us siblings. I remembered this incident at the hospital when Guruji came and stood behind me after the condolence meeting.

After the condolence meeting I saw the smoke going towards the sky. It did not spread around but went speedily higher and higher up until it was beyond the reach of my eyes. The sun had set. The red hue of the western twilight appeared as though a red carpet was spread out as a welcome for my mother. I gestured with my eyes to Guruji drawing his attention to the rising smoke and how God had spread out a red carpet in the skies to welcome my mother. Guruji stared at the endless expanse of the universe in wonder. I watched him as he stood silent with dampened eyes.

We siblings were about to return home along with our relatives when all of a sudden there was a huge sound of thunder. Everyone stopped short. For a moment all were aghast and looked at the skies, and guess what? It had started pouring down heavily. It was not the rainy season. Summer was just about to start. The sun had been scorching hot since morning. Since lighting the pyre there was not a single black cloud in the sky. And now for ten minutes it was a heavy down pour illuminated by lightning amidst sounds of thunder. All were stunned into silence, experiencing this magical occurrence.

There was a question in my mind. It was just this simple, innocent mind that was going to miss the mother's loving presence in the coming days. I felt that mother had gone straight up towards heaven. A red carpet had been spread to welcome her. Has she got a place in heaven? She will surely get a place there. Throughout her life she had struggled for the welfare of the people, for the upliftment of the tribal society. She would definitely be rewarded for her virtues with a place in the heaven; I was sure.

Still, I couldn't stop myself and asked Guruji, 'After death does God really give place to good people in heaven?

Do you think my mother has found a place in heaven? Wasn't it a welcoming gesture that the skies were illuminated like a red carpet and there was so much sound when she reached there? Please tell me Guruji.'

Guruji was still and remained silent. He must have felt that I wouldn't be satisfied with a succinct answer. Nor was this a time or a place for a long discourse. But I could not help it. Until I got an answer I would not rest in peace; Guruji was aware of this.

Once again I implored, 'Guruji, please say something; please talk.'

Guruji looked into my eyes and said quietly, 'Yes, your mother must have got a place in heaven.'

I knew instantly that he had said that to console me, to pacify me. And once again, without a word, I kept looking pointedly into his eyes.

Guruji could not ignore me and said, 'We will talk about death some other time. Right now, please relax.'

Reminiscing about my mother with the visitors, I did not realise how twelve-thirteen days had passed by since her demise. As per the Hindu customs on the third, tenth, eleventh, twelfth and thirteenth day various rituals were performed under the supervision of the *pandits*. On the fourteenth day there was a big lunch programme for those in the society, relatives, etc. That day the ceremony lasted till eight in the evening. Around two thousand people must have had food with us on that day. In the last fourteen days Guruji had visited us two to three times. Out of curiosity, I had asked him for information on various subjects, like death and life thereafter. Of the information given by Guruji the one that I remember the most is this.

When lying on his deathbed a human being aspires to see his entire life, with its good and bad memories, like a movie. It is difficult to comprehend the extraordinary power of the human mind at this juncture as during the short intermediary period we can see our entire life unfolding before us. The essence of the entire lifetime is absorbed by the soul in the form of an imprint of this life. Just as a fruit falls to the ground when the stalk gets weak, similarly when a person's weakness surpasses its lowermost limit, while the body is in the unconscious state, the soul departs from the body. Indian sages visualised the soul in the form of a bright white flame of light.

With regard to how death happens, as per the writings of honourable sages, a person experiences acute uneasiness, pain and discomfort for some time prior to his death. This is because the life element in his various organs fuses together. The life element from each cell gets pulled out and converges towards a common point. A person undergoes severe pain during the process of death which he is unable to express due to weakness or disease. Nearing death he first passes through a comatose stage. During the unconscious state, in the moments of acute suffering, he waits for death to take over. In the circumstances, the process of death must mean a gift from providence......

Once the soul leaves the body, the body goes into a deep sleep — the way an exhausted person, after a hard day's work, let goes of himself on seeing a soft bed! But he does not attain peace instantaneously. It takes almost a month for the departed soul to find peace. This is because temptations in life continue to affect him for a while even after death, although they gradually fade away. I remember reading that after leaving the physical body the departed soul continues to linger around its lifeless remains. It continues this way in its vicinity trying to once again find its way into the body, until the last rites are performed. The tremendous attraction of the departed soul for the physical body is the main reason for this. Similarly things like clothes, glasses, etc. used by the body during its life time also holds attraction for the departed soul. But since the body is dead, the desires and aspirations of the soul that could be gratified only through the medium of the physical body remain unfulfilled. This is why when a person dies, we pray for peace of the departed soul. In our Hindu religion, after performing the last rites we observe a number of systematic rituals meant for attainment of peace for the departed soul. Various rituals are performed on the third, tenth, eleventh, twelfth thirteenth and fourteenth day after death in order that the soul is released from the worldly attractions and moves towards divine peace.

As regards the concept of heaven and hell, as per our holy books one who does bad deeds goes to hell and the one with good virtuous deeds gets a place in heaven after death. But this subject is extremely complicated and there are different schools of thought having their own interpretations. Various intellectuals and experts in the field have put forward their own theories. But a common binding thread is that in life we fear the outcome of bad deeds and if during our lifetime we inculcate a belief that good deeds will definite bring about good results, then we will surely choose to do good rather than bad, and this will facilitate creating a higher quality of human character.

At last, the rituals of the fourteenth day were over. All of us were dead tired but all the same there was feeling of satisfaction. People from various fields had visited us today.

The many social activities that my mother was involved in were the subject of conversation throughout the day. Relatives and close family members sat relaxing in the drawing room. We were discussing the praises showered on mother by various people throughout the day. Listening to all this talk gave me a feeling of immense gratification. Once again I felt very lucky to have been born to such a mother. After a while the crowd dispersed with only two of us, Guruji and me, remaining behind in the large room. It was the first time I had noticed so much adulation for a person after her death. A person with noble deeds gets any amount of fame and honour during his life time and his death too does not put a stop to this. The person remains alive in the minds of people even after death in the form of his selfless service and continues to earn the same honour and respect. Isn't that amazing?

I gave me a great feeling to hear the tributes being paid to my mother and accept them. Nevertheless I yearned to hear something authentic from Guruji.

I prompted him, 'Guruji, as you said the other day, has my mother really found a place in heaven?'

Guruji too spoke at length about the selfless nature of my mother. He elaborated on how he had discerned the intricate shades of her character during his many interactions with her. Her serious nature, her yearning for knowledge by going deep into any subject, her way of finding analytical solution to any problem in life, her intrinsic desire to cooperate with anyone without hurting him, etc, and the memorable moments he had experienced with her – Guruji went on and on ....

I listened in silence and felt waves of happiness flow through me. It was around eleven thirty at night but while listening to Guruji I was as usual unaware of the passing of time.

The discussion led to the subject of death and the miraculous happenings taking place after death. Guruji spoke as if he had seen death from close quarters or had experienced it. In the course of the discussion Guruji put a question to me.

'Tell me, Kama, haven't you experienced the near death moments when you were admitted at the Hinduja hospital?'

Whilst resting on the sofa I was once again thrown back in the past memories. While those experiences passed one by one before my eyes, I didn't realise when sleep came over me.

JAWS OF CANCER

Since the last few days, or rather the last few years, I would get pain in both my breasts. When my son was born I could not feed him because there wasn't much milk. But some days after my delivery I had undergone a lot of pain. I still remembered that. So I thought that the pain that I was getting now since the last few years must be due to the same reason. But now my son was studying in the tenth standard. After so many years the pain had erupted once again. I would always feel feverish. Thinking that it must be due to daily travel and exhaustion I ignored it initially and carried on as usual. Eventually both my breasts had developed lumps and their increasing size was causing me pain in the entire breasts. My job was going on as usual. When I felt more feverish or exhausted I would take a day or two off once in fifteen or twenty days and take rest. As soon as I felt better, I would resume. After a while I felt some change in my skin texture and unexpectedly the nipples started oozing. And that is when I got scared.

I had read in the newspapers and journals that although the percentage of breast cancer patients had reduced in the US, statistically the number of deaths on account of breast cancer was expected to be 39620 by 2013. I had also read that only five to ten per cent of the cases were genetically transferred. As per the survey in the US about eighty five per cent of cancer patients did not have any history of cancer in the family. I thought our Indian lifestyle differed totally from the American lifestyle. Their eating habits and ours were different. What holds good for them may not necessarily hold good for us. I had all along thought that the pain I had to endure due to my feeding problem at the time of delivery had now relapsed and I was getting the same pain again. I had also read that lumps do not always indicate cancer. Still when I realised the problem of lymph nodes then that scared me. I started feeling that now it was already too late. I was in two minds. On the one hand I felt that I would not get this terrible disease at such a young age and on the other I feared the worst.

Once when I was suddenly tired and feeling feverish, I took leave for a couple of days to rest. On that day Guruji came home casually to meet me. I was lying down like a sick person. I told Guruji everything about my illness. Guruji sternly reprimanded me for the delay in going to the doctor and told me to see a lady doctor by evening.

I went to my lady doctor immediately in the evening. She gave me a patient hearing and referred me to a well-known doctor and tried to reduce my anxiety by explaining to me the basics.

Next day morning I visited the referred specialist. I had specially called Guruji and met the doctor along with him. I didn't know what to tell and how to tell the doctor. I was truly scared. Momentarily I thought I was swinging like a pendulum between life and death. Doctor read the note from the earlier doctor and told me to get the biopsy done, followed by other pathological tests. As usual the doctor advised me not to get scared; everything will be fine, nothing to worry, etc. Then she told me to wait outside and gave some instructions to her assistant. With heavy steps, as if in a trance, I came out of the cabin and sat on a bench. After some time a nurse-like assistant came to us and said that the doctor had called this relative of yours. Without wasting any time Guruji, like a close relative, entered the doctor's cabin. The doctor must have apprised Guruji about the seriousness of the disease and the biopsy and other pathological tests to be done prior to starting the treatment. Guruji came from the cabin carrying two printed forms in which the patient's name and other details had to be filled in. I remember Guruji signing on it after taking my signature.

Biopsy is a minor surgery. A tissue sample is removed from the affected area of the body and sent to the pathologist for specialised opinion. This biopsy report takes around four-five days.

When I heard the doctor ask for biopsy test, I realised the seriousness of my illness. There was a terrible disease in my body. I was petrified when I heard the word biopsy. When Guruji was called inside by the doctor I knew something was serious. When he went in I could not control my tears. The nurse came near me. She was old. She held me close and tried to comfort me.

There are many pathological tests to be done after the biopsy. Blood cell count gives the detailed pathological reports of white blood cells, red blood cells, level of haemoglobin, level of hematoint, platelets, etc.

Blood chemistries test indicates levels of liver enzymes, potassium chloride, urea nitrogen, calcium etc. which enables doctors to ascertain the conditions of the bones and the kidney. There are several other tests too; for example, bone scan, breast MRI, breast physical examination, breast self-examination, blood marker tests, chest x-rays, digital tom synthesis, etc.

Guruji took the signed paper from me, signed on the side and handed it over to the doctor. After checking with me the doctor scheduled the biopsy test for the next day.

Guruji told me to call mother the next day to accompany me to the hospital.

Next day, before leaving for the biopsy at the hospital, both mother and I clung to each other and broke down. Mother said 'Child, its God's wish. This is our fate. Don't lose hope. God is kind and let's hope everything is going to be fine.' My elder brother, who is a doctor, also made it a point to come this time. This was a great comfort to me.

During Biopsy surgery a small tissue sample is taken out from the affected area of the body and sent to the specialised opinion. Generally it takes around four-five days to get biopsy report.

Your doctor plays prime role while handling such cases and planning for treatment. Recommendations for proper treatment depends upon various factors options and recommendations depend on several factors, including; the stage of the tumour, patient's age, general health and menopausal status of the patient. Some tumours are small and grow fast; some are large and grow slowly. The main aim of surgery is to remove all of the visible cancer. Sometimes it may happen that the microscopic cells can be left behind in some part of body. Which may require another surgery! Therefore, many times specialist doctors recommend chemotherapy before surgery. In specific situations, it may happen even after surgery the recurrence of the disease. In case of early stage of breast cancer and to lower the risk of recurrence and to get rid of any remaining cancer cells patient has to undergo chemotherapy. Treatment given after surgery is called adjuvant therapy. When surgery is not possible, it is called inoperable.

It is also very important that one should also get well-informed by doctors regarding symptoms and side effects during treatment. When you have to fight such a disease you must clear up all your hidden questions and find out time to discuss with doctors. You have to get more information about treatment planning. A doctor who specializes in treating cancer with surgery called as a surgical oncologist. Radiation therapy is usually given daily by a doctor called a radiation oncologist. This goes for number of weeks. This help get rid of any remaining cancer cells in the breast or elsewhere in the breast.

NEAR DEATH EXPERIENCE

I was watching the waves go on a rampage at the Worli sea face in Mumbai. The waves of emotions crossing my mind would not let me relax. Now what? What does the future hold? I had never imagined myself grappling with such a terrible disease at such a young age. I was in Mumbai for the past one week. The district doctor had asked for biopsy report. I had been called and apprised fully about the disease. I was suffering from breast cancer and it had reached the second stage. This was now confirmed. My brother, who was a doctor, had checked all the reports. As per the doctor, the WBC RBC platelet count was not satisfactory. My brother discussed the case with the specialist and it was decided to immediately start the treatment at the Hinduja Hospital. My mother, brother and I, all three of us came to Mumbai and I underwent radiation twice in the week. The doctor was going to let us know about the schedule for the chemotherapy program. The nurses and the doctor told me that chemotherapy was a very successful form of treatment. There was no need to worry. Nowadays this ailment has become very common. Our stressful lifestyle is a main cause of this disease. There was no end to the advice and information being fed into me. But in all this discussion there was one major issue – that of amputation. If the disease did not respond to radiation and chemotherapy, and if the lumps increased, breast amputation would be the only option. It would have to be done to save life. The thought terrified me. The pathological reports were unfavourable and some cells/hormones were already damaged. Production of new healthy cells took a while. In the circumstances it became necessary to start implementing the chemotherapy schedule immediately. With this if the disease could be kept under control, the next step of amputation could be avoided. I had also heard about radiation and chemotherapy damaging other useful cells of the body which could result in thinning of hair, changes in the skin colour or even brain complications leading to loss of memory.

Hinduja hospital is right next to the sea shore. Horrific thoughts occupied my mind as I sat on the stone wall watching the thunderous swash of waves. When I left for Mumbai, Guruji had come to see me off at the station. I was sitting inside the compartment in a completely dejected state along with my mother and brother.

Guruji advised, 'when God creates problems he also gives us the strength to overcome them'.

With assurance in his eyes he continued, 'Nothing will happen to you. Live with conviction and you will get well and come back.'

I said, 'Guruji, I don't want to die, at least not for now. Let my little one complete his studies. Let me live at least till he finishes his education. Guruji, do something!'

Guruji repeated with confidence, 'Nothing will happen to you. You will get well and come back.'

Now sitting at the seashore Guruji's words were constantly ringing in my ears. Like an assurance from an enlightened soul, an angel, they were a source of great comfort to me. By now I had prepared myself to undergo any treatment.

One session of radiation and chemotherapy was scheduled every week. As advised by Guruji I would recite *Hanuman Chalisa* both morning and evening. On the day of the treatment I would call up Guruji in the morning. He would recite *Hanuman Chalisa* over the cell phone and I would recite it with him from my hospital bed. I experienced the presence of God through the medium of *Hanuman Chalisa* and the angel was at my side in the form of Guruji.

Life is the most precious thing in the world. We cannot imagine life without body. When a dreadful disease like cancer affects the body only then we realise the true value of a healthy and safe body. When I was diagnosed as suffering from cancer that is what created an awareness of death in me. Life started appearing more beautiful than ever before. Before I came to know of my cancer, I had never felt afraid of death. But nor did I value life. Life did not hold any particular attraction for me. The world is so large. All are born to go through life. My simplistic concept of life was that whoever was born into this world was going to live.

For seven continuous months I was under treatment at the Hinduja Hospital. The knowledge that I had cancer and that death was at close quarters gave me fresh aspirations about living my life. This thought created a love for life within me. I had decided to fight my cancer. No matter what my condition, I was going to fight death till the end. I had decided to defeat it. Cancer taught me the value of life. Now I knew the worth of my people, the people around me. I became aware of my standing in other people's lives, of how much they cared for me. I came to know who were mine and who weren't. That only blood relations belonged to we had proved to be a wrong notion. There are others too who do far more for us that even our own blood relations, who are always at hand in the times of need.

My mother and brother both took great pains to nurse and look after me during my illness. Guruji came to Mumbai once. On arriving at Hinduja when he set his eyes on me, they were filled with tears. Chemotherapy had taken its toll on my body which now looked like a parched tree. The glow on my face, sparkle in the eyes and exuberance in speech were all gone. All this touched Guruji's heart. Someone other than my close relatives coming all the way from eight hundreds kilometres to meet and enquire about my ailment was a matter of great surprise for my mother and brother, and they were very pleased. I too felt very happy. When confronted by an incurable disease, each and every person coming to meet us, before leaving, gives us the strength to live life. At least for a while the mind drifts away from the thought of the sickness and pain, and once again there is the will to live one's life. Their good will snatches us away from the jaws of death. We realise how many people in the world we could connect to, and how important it is to remain connected with people. While discovering the mystery of death we also discover the mystery of human emotions and feelings.

Though cancer had weakened me physically I did not think the disease had affected my intellect in any way. Although the body had turned weak and dull, I had not lost my hair. I looked physically tired but when I saw myself in the mirror I did not notice any hair loss as I was given to understand earlier. Its colour too was lustrous black and not dull at all. This was no doubt a miracle because whenever I asked the doctors about it they could never give me a satisfactory reply. They called it an exceptional case. Whenever such things happened *Hanuman Chalisa* would instantly ring in my years. I would be grateful to God and would reassure myself that I would no die of this disease. In a lighter vein Guruji would say, 'You don't have any cancer. In cancer you lose your hair. Have lost any of yours?' In spite of this incurable disease Guruji would bring a smile to my tired face.

Guruji had got a book for me. It was about the experiences narrated by people who had fought and defeated cancer. Besides medical treatment a cancer patient needed positive vibrations from others. They needed reassurance. During treatment the pain of injections was unbearable. The medicines had many side effects. There were unpleasant effects of chemotherapy. There was a feeling of burning sensation in the body all along. There was no taste for food. My own people at my side were my only source of positive energy. Mother and brother would always try to humour me. When Guruji spoke to me I felt as if he had forgotten that he was speaking to a cancer patient. He was simple and humorous, and would share jokes with me. It went a long way in helping me forget about my condition.

I was getting increasingly tired of my repeated check-ups. But now after seven long months the pathological reports were quite encouraging and finally the doctors declared that I was now out of danger.

At last I was out of the Hinduja Hospital and Mumbai. I had experienced death face to face and it had now released me. I was totally burnt out. The doctors advised me to take rest at home for one to two months and then I could eat, drink, or do whatever I wished and enjoy life. "Now you are a normal healthy person like any of us," they said.

Thank God, thank Guruji! Along with God how many others had I to be grateful to, I could not fathom. Mother and brother were with me all throughout. Doctors, nurses, cleaners and the person in a blue outfit who came every day and enquired about me – all of them had become a part of my life. They had been the source of so much strength to me. I could never thank them enough; I was at a loss of words. I bade them good bye with teary eyes and a heavy heart. In fake anger the cleaner said to me, 'Beta, I warn you. I don't want to see you on this bed ever again!' I bent down and touched his feet and felt his warm tears on my back.

I had found my answer as to why I had distanced myself from spirituality.

Beta: Generally youngers are fondly called by Seniors with love, In Hindu culture.

LONELINESS

My son was now growing up and due to appear for his tenth standard. Since childhood it was single parenting for him; I was his mother and father as well. His clothes and toys were all as per his liking. But now he has turned out to be so obstinate that I am exasperated. In summer we had gone to buy a cap for him. They were from rupees hundred onwards but he chose a branded one for rupees three fifty. I was the only earning member but could afford it though. But so what? I was against it. Such an expensive cap! Not only that, he invariably opted for expensive things, right from innerwear to the bag that he carried to school. At home he would get annoyed over minor things. I would come home tired and pamper him in every way but in spite of this he would misbehave with me.

The vices of the father had started reflecting in the child. I was getting increasingly obsessed by the fact that it was the same blood of the cruel father that was now flowing through Shyam. To me his arrogant and angry nature was a constant reminder of his father's barbarism. I had place the lot of hopes and aspirations on Shyam, had nurtured so many dreams around him. Like any other mother I too had my normal expectations from him. Every mother wants her child to have a good character. In my prime time I had faced hardships with courage. Now too my grit to overcome adversities has not dimmed. In future my entire life was going to be judged based on how Shyam turns out to be, on his character and success. It is an accepted norm that making a success of my son's life would be the benchmark to my own bright future. And making him successful was no doubt going to prove an uphill task .... and I am aware of it.

But the thought of my old age made me restless. I could not imagine what would happen if Shyam grew up in his father's footsteps!

As per a research report published in an international journal, Cerebral Cortex, it has been observed that children brought up without a father figure display abnormal social interaction tendencies. As compared to children brought up by both the parents, the children brought up without a father were found to have a permanently altered brain structure. Such children were found to be extremely irritable and obstinate by nature. The behavioural deficits observed were consistent with human studies of children raised without father.

Although this was the inference drawn from an international study, as a mother it was important for me to go beyond this and see how I could help him improve. He was this way due to his single parenting; I was quite sure about that. But I was not prepared to accept that he would never change. I told him about the ways of mediation, but couldn't explain to him that effectively. Nevertheless I had to resolve this serious issue and so decided to consult Guruji. I had complete faith in him that he would suggest a perfect solution to this problem. I called Guruji over and narrated the entire problem to him.

Guruji said, 'That's true. Single parenting is the main issue. Such weird behaviour is generally found in children brought up without a father. They are always irritable, get very angry and aggressive. This severely affects their academic performance. All this is due to a feeling of loneliness. This may be considered a kind of mental illness. But don't think of it as a curse. First of all you will have to think of ways to get rid of his loneliness. For this you will have to find time in your daily routine to develop a rapport with him. He should be made to speak out. It will be necessary to get close to him emotionally and take a stock of what is going on in his mind.

A lonely person keeps churning his thoughts and does not find a vent for an outburst. The thoughts remain stagnant with him like stored water without an outlet.

As for single parenting, your immediate concern in the role of a mother should be to check upon his way thinking. His thoughts should facilitate the process of character building. Developing a sense of discretion is tantamount to character building or character growth. He needs plenty of love and compassion to deal with his own irritability and obstinacy. So try and sympathise with him. Gradually as he realises your love, affection and sympathy for him, his hatred and anger will start subsiding. Explain to him the values of integrity and moral strength. Once he imbibes the values of love, kindness, cooperation, dedication in his behaviour then his mental agitation will come down. Right now he is caught in a conflict between right and wrong and is unable to distinguish between the two. This is also called ethical dilemma. To inspire moral principles in him you may have to take the aid of happenings in the bygone days, religious stories, good or bad incidents from history, fables with morals, etc. which will give him a new perspective of thinking when he is in solitude. He will not waste his time while away over unproductive thoughts. He will improve his will power. Today he is experiencing helplessness on account of his lack of faith in himself, ambivalence and his lack of confidence. He considers aggression as the only way to achieve happiness or whatever else, and is unaware that things can be achieved peacefully by strengthening ourselves with determination, commitment, self-sacrifice and perseverance.

Imitating others is the intrinsic nature of small children. Therefore elders and teachers should keep moral values in mind when in the company of children. Children imbibe whatever they see. As long as we ourselves do not practice moral behaviour it is not possible to make children imbibe it. Every person has his own typical mentality. Along with his strengths he also nurtures weaknesses. Your ability to handle a situation depends on your strengths and weaknesses. It is this ability that enables you to overcome the various mental traumas and critical emotional issues. So through our behaviour we must convey the message to our children so that they, by using their discretion and by listening to their conscience with faith and confidence, develop the ability to take the right decisions.

Afterwards during the course of discussions, many things related with day to day difficulties faced were discussed with guruji. Once I said we felt insulted, when people give us inferior treatment. What to react?"

His answer was as like this. If anyone abuses us the natural reaction is bound to emerge within us. And that reaction, if made vocal, would inevitably lead to an argument. So now you try this. You know that if you react it creates unpleasantness. This is a fact. So control yourself and refrain from reacting. Others will try to instigate you into reacting. They look for entertainment in your reaction and will compel you to react. You try and do just the opposite. He said that what was said above happens to be the rule. Do not react and watch the result of not reacting to their comments. Disappointed, they will find new ways of harassing you, and you continue to practise the same rule of non-reaction. This of course will require a lot of courage and patience on your part. I wondered how I could garner so much courage and patience. He said that was the reason that he had used the word 'spirituality' at the outset. It is spirituality that makes us strong - physically and spiritually.

MY PHD

The subject of my project was 'A study to promote public participation in eradication of liquor abuse and awareness program amongst Tribal (*Adiwasis*) in remote area of this backward district'. This is one of the two hundred and fifty most backward districts in India. As the tribal community comprises of thirty eight per cent of the total population, there was tremendous scope to do work on this subject.

As I myself hailed from this district, for many years I had this acute yearning to understand and study the tribal society and its lifestyle, the tribals' daily struggle to make a living and bring it before the world. But that remained just a wish. During discussions amongst our friends on the atrocities committed on the tribals, educational and health facilities in the remote tribal areas and such other preferred topics, I would express my desire to do PhD in the subject. But they would make fun of my dream or the subject would taper off in a lighter vein. This is what happened many a times. People opined that the tribals I was referring to stayed in remote places; doing their individual surveys, travelling hundreds of miles in the remote places in the forests and interacting with them on a regular basis was an extremely hazardous job.

Once during one of his visits at my home, whilst having tea, Guruji glanced at the newspaper. He came across the news item that twelve tribals in a remote area had died after consuming liquor. The news pained Guruji very much. He was very disturbed and said, ' The lack of education amongst the tribal is main cause of liquor abuse. Tribal are not aware of hazards to their lives because of liquor consumption. Dr Prakash Amte is very active socially in that region. He has done tremendous work in the field of education, health and upliftment of their living standards. He has also been awarded the Magsaysay award. He has devoted his entire life for the upliftment of the tribal. Such efforts are the need of the day. Many more development programmes are to be implemented. Government agencies and NGOs are doing the job to the satisfaction. But, it becomes very vast and difficult due to deep forest area and inconveniency to reach every tribal habitation. Aren't you from the same district? And also a post graduate! The only difference between you and them is that you have evolved. You are educated and have come up in life. Don't you feel like doing something for your own community living in the remote places and is extremely backward?'

Guruji had said exactly what was in my mind. I have been cherishing the dream of doing something in this field. I remembered the words of Bharat Ratna Dr A P J Abdul Kalam - 'Dream! Make a habit of dreaming. You have to dream before your dreams can come true.' It was my dream for many years to make research in social problems in tribal community. God must have sent this gentleman to provoke me into fulfilling it.

I said, 'Guruji, for so many years I have been thinking of a research study in a subject of social science and complete

---

Hon. Dr Prakash Amte (Magsaysay award winner) is renown personality dedicated his life for the welfare of tribal in remote area.

doctorate. But nothing can be materialized for some or other reason and I had to give it up. Now with the God grace, I think, the proper time came.'

Guruji replied, 'Very good, excellent idea!'.

I was very happy for a moment looking in to a hope of doing research work in my favourite subject and I murmured my thanks.

Then Guruji said, 'See, take it seriously and start your research work without loss of time. Something new can come out from your study; which can throw light on some hidden facts of tribal lives. The study can decide further the line of action and by the way you can get PhD too in the subject of their liquor eradication and a subject of your choice'.

I was hesitant, 'but that is not so simple.'

Guruji explained, 'No work is easy. We have to make it easy by our hard work and perseverance. And where there is a will, there is a way.'

I still had my doubts. 'Will I, all by myself, able to concentrate simultaneously on the various activities like collecting data from remote places hundreds of miles from the district, conducting interviews, reviewing the work done by government and semi-government (NGO) institutions like the schemes implemented by them, if these schemes are proving beneficial to the remote tribal areas and such other things and manage to complete the entire project?'

Guruji replied, 'The project has to be completed by you and you alone. But I will always be there to help you whenever you need me.'

'Oh, really?' I exclaimed.

Guruji was positive. 'Yes, absolutely sure! You go ahead with the formalities of registration, synopsis, etc. You have my full support.'

'Okay, Guruji, I will get on with it from tomorrow itself,' said I.

On hearing his words offering me full support I was instantly filled with exuberance as if a lightening spark was passing through me. Guruji's words were invigorating and I had experienced that many a times earlier. I felt that the cent per cent support for my PhD implied that he had virtually ordered me to do my PhD. My dream of so many years would now come true. My self-confidence was awakened. Now I was truly prepared for any amount of hard work. I was ready to throw myself into it wholeheartedly. Guruji had displayed full faith in my intellect. He had discerned my trait of fully giving me up in work. With his encouragement now the PhD project was no longer a wish or an ambition but it had now become a responsibility; because Guruji was so true to his word and determined that once he had made up his mind he would never retrace nor would he allow others to do so no matter what the consequences. I was overcome with emotion. Silently I offered my obeisance to Hanumanji, and thanked him and the messenger of God in the form of Guruji as well.

The letter from Nagpur University was received by us just four days back. It was signed by the Acting Vice Chancellor. The letter was accompanied by an invitation card. The card extended a cordial invitation to me to be present along with my family members and grace the occasion. Bharat Ratna Dr A P J Abdul Kalam was to be the Chief Guest at the function while the great scientist Dr Vijay Bhatkar, best known as the architect of India's national initiative in supercomputing, was slated to attend the function. He was to be conferred the D.Litt. Hon degree. The function was scheduled for 3 pm and a number of high profile people from Nagpur were expected to attend.

On receiving the invite I was absolutely overwhelmed. The moment that I was looking forward to for the last so many years was at last here. The dream of many years was about to be fulfilled and moreover I was going to receive the PhD from such an acclaimed person. My dream was being fulfilled by such an erudite personality, who had so often said, 'Dream, dreams come true!' In my case my dream was coming true. When one is ecstatic it is a state that cannot remain hidden. I was so restless and unable to think coherently. Whom do I tell, what do I do? Which relatives would accompany me to the function? Whom should I take along… etc.

At the outset I called up Guruji. 'Hello Sir, good news!'

Guruji asked, 'Oh Kama, tell me quickly, what is it?'

I said, 'Guruji, it's the centenary celebration program of the convocation on 26th September at 3 in the afternoon. And I… I'm going to get my PhD.'

Guruji shrieked from the other end, 'Wow! Congratulations!!'

I said, 'Guruji, I just received the invitation card. Thank God! Thanks Guruji. I'm so happy, Guruji……. Guruji, you are coming for the function.'

Guruji replied, 'Of course. This is a fulfilment of my dream too! I'm definitely coming. Once again congratulations, Kama!'

I said, 'Thanks Guruji. Thank you so much.'

Navratri had begun yesterday, on 26th September 2014. Today was the second day of Navratri. Right from the morning one could feel the pure and sacred sensations in the air. An idol of *Durgadevi* was set up at the crossing adjacent to the society where we stay. Since early morning soft sounds of *bhajans* and songs floated in the air from the huge speakers put up for the occasion lending a strong auspicious flavour to the ambience. The ambience had become religious and sacred. Isn't it true that when we are happy and pure from within the same feelings are reflected back from the universe? The entire atmosphere appears to be auspicious. I too decided to finish all the morning chores, get dressed, finish the daily prayers and rituals, and start the day after paying a visit to the goddess in our neighbourhood.

Durga Puja is the festival celebrated since ancient time all over India. *Durga* is known to be *'Aadi Shakti'* the supreme goddess by the Hindus. By killing 'Mahisasura' the demon, she restored peace on earth. Durga Puja celebration comes in the month of *Ashwin* as per Hindu calendar. As per the Gregorian calendar it generally falls in the months between September and October. Durga Puja symbolizes the victory of good over evil.

As per the plans the day began after visiting the goddess and thanking her profusely. My doctor brother and

---

Durgadevi – A Goddess Durga,

Bhajan – Religious poems and songs

Durgapuja – Durga Puja festival marks the victory of Goddess Durga over the evil buffalo demon Mahisasura. The festival celebrated since ancient time all over India which is the mark of worship to the Hindu goddess Durga

Aadi Shakti – The deity is considered as the Power beyond this universe. She is the active energy that both creates and dissolves the entire universe.

Ashwin – The name of seventh month according to Hindu Calendar

sister-in-law had arrived from the village. I, along with my son, Shyam and a friend of mine reached the venue of the function in my brother's car at around three in the afternoon. A huge *shamiyana* had been erected on the university playground. A red carpet had been spread out right from the entrance of the *shamiyana* to the stage. Seating arrangements were made in the entire *shamiyana*. The front two rows from the stage were reserved for the VIP guests. The next three rows were for one thousand PhD students. Next to the rows for the PhD students a special section was reserved for the principals and guides from various colleges. Thereafter seating was reserved for the outstanding graduation and post-graduation students, and the remaining seats were open to invitees, namely parents, relatives, journalists, professors of colleges, lecturers, etc. A number of TV screens were put up in order that the program on the stage could be clearly visible from far. Two big screens were put up at the end of the *shamiyana* as well as on either sides of the stage. The sound system was excellent. There were speakers all over the place and soft notes of *Shehnai* floated in the air. All the bamboo pillars in the shamiyana were decorated with marigold flowers. A board saying 'Convocation Centenary Celebrations' was attractively displayed on the dais and the dais was lavishly decorated with flowers. The entire venue was sprayed with a pleasing perfume. The overall ambience was exotic and joyful.

---

shamiyana – Shamiyana is a popular Indian ceremonial tent shelter or awning, commonly used for outdoor functions.

Shehnai – It is a musical instrument & made out of wood. Its sound is thought to create and maintain a sense of auspiciousness and sanctity

Volunteers were seen assisting the guests with the seating. They ushered in the VIPs and the students to their delegated seats. Some of them were being helped to reach their seats. I took my seat in the PhD students' area as directed while my brother along with the others sat in the places allocated to them. There was excitement on everyone's face. There was interest about the program, how it was going to turn out. Volunteers and the police were seen hustling, and at times running, here and there. We could not follow what exactly they were saying to one another. They would check arrangements on the dais or at times check the mike. 'Hello, mike testing, one, two, three, four…. mike testing please!'

Most of the honourable guests had arrived by now. The first two rows were fully occupied by the VIPs. The entire *shamiyana* was now full. The police officers were roaming around as usual with tense expressions on their faces. Some were speaking on their walkie-talkies while others were using their mobile phones. I turned back and looked far behind. The entire *shamiyana* was full but I could not spot any familiar face. May be it was not possible to recognise anyone from that far. I could not see where Guruji was sitting and that made me a bit anxious. But I was sure Guruji would definitely be present at this important event. My gut feeling was reassuring; he was sure to be there somewhere. And that would temporarily quieten my restlessness.

No matter how big or small an event is and how well it has been organised, at the final moment there is always a rush and chaos at the organisers. And that's what was observed here too. In a pleasant and composed voice a woman was making announcements over the loud speakers. 'The Chief Guest will be arriving in a short while.' No sooner the announcement was made a group of women in traditional Maharashtrian attire carrying an *arati thali* in their hands rushed towards the main entrance of the *shamiyana*. In keeping with my inherent nature I gave in to my worries. The entrance gate was quite a distance from the stage and the women will have to be there before the Chief Guest to welcome him. I was restless and continuously kept a watch on the entrance gate behind me. It was 3 o'clock. Within moments a motorcade appeared at the entrance gate. The police officers encircled the entire gate. Dr APJ Abdul Kalam along with other dignitaries appeared at the entrance gate. As per the Indian custom, particularly the Maharashtrian custom, five women welcomed Bharat Ratna Dr APJ AbdulKalam with an arati. The honourable organisers, the Vice Chancellor and other senior personnel accompanied the Chief Guest to the stage.

As per the usual practice observed in such events, the program began with a welcome song, followed by the welcoming ceremony for the Chief Guest and then the lighting of the lamp, indicating the start of the event. Speeches were delivered by the honourable guests. I was so excited and impatient, and did not recollect any of the speeches. In a state of ecstasy I was not myself. I was in no mood to listen to any of the speakers except of course Bharat Ratna Dr APJ Abdul Kalam, who started his speech by reading out from a paper in Marathi and then continued in English.

"Congratulations to all the students of the Nagpur University," Dr A P J Abdul Kalam, the former President of India, started his speech in Marathi-local language. The

---

aarti – A prayer or a song that accompanies a lamp for waving.
Thali – A tray equipped with a lamp for waving and other puja material.

name of our university is Rashtrasant Tukdoji Maharaj Nagpur University, generally referred to as Nagpur University. Today, Friday, the 26th September 2014 the famous scientist, Bharat Ratna Dr A P J Abdul Kalam was presiding as the Chief Guest at the centenary celebrations of the convocation.

Today around one thousand students of the Nagpur University were to be conferred PhD degrees. I was so very lucky to be one amongst those. 'Dream big and soar to uncharted heights.' These encouraging words had been the source of inspiration to countless Indian youths. I too was one of them inspired by the words of Dr A P J Abdul Kalam. And today I was to receive my PhD from him. Of the few happy occasions in my life this one topped the list. I was really very lucky and today I was acutely aware of it. It was quite a few months since I had submitted my thesis. I had put in great efforts during the preparations for completing the project for PhD. The people with me had been a great help too. Apart from my university guide, the main person who stood by me was my Guruji.

I was required to visit the far away remote tribal locations at odd times, take interviews of the tribal, individually as well as in groups, sometimes in the very early mornings or late in the evenings or nights. Without the assistance of Guruji perhaps it would have been very tough for me. The tribal were not found at home during the day. Once they were out for work in the jungles or the farms, they returned only in the evenings. Also since my subject was concerning relief from alcoholism, the nature of my work was complicated and involved observing their behaviour at home or outside when not under the influence of alcohol, or otherwise in the evenings, take their interviews, etc. It was necessary to talk to them in order to ascertain what was driving them to drinking. Were they drinking out of frustration or poverty, or was it just a means of recreation? Was it because the small village/settlement did not have any recreational facilities? Or was it in order to be in line with others in the neighbourhood? Or they want to forget of their poverty? For some even two square meals a day was hard to come by. Did they drink so that they could have a good night's sleep? Instead of struggling with the circumstances did they believe that they could overcome the situation by giving in to drinking? Or did they want to run away or keep aloof from reality and so indulged in drinking? Did they give it so much thought before indulging in drinking or did they do so out of ignorance? There were myriad questions that had to be answered and for this group discussions had to be organised. For this assistance of police or the village head was required. At times we even had to catch hold of some tribal ring leader and request him to get all the tribal in one place. It would definitely not have been possible for a woman like me to manage all that. Guruji was a God sent angel and would manage everything for me. The hilarious part was that when we had the so called respected police or the village head or any social worker to accompany us, many a times they themselves would be in a fully inebriated state. And that meant we had to start by counselling these people first. Sometimes they would grumble at our frequent requests for assistance and we had no choice but to endure it. Also the tribal stayed in groups of thirty to forty houses each, which would be around two kilometres from one another. The people staying in the different groups maintained somewhat different lifestyles.

There was disparity in their familial needs, skills at various jobs, distances from places of work and their typical lifestyles. For example, some people would hunt and feed themselves while others worked and earned money to make a living, while still others did farming and survived on bulbs, roots and whatever other foods were available. It is on account of these differences in lifestyles, needs and habits that they stayed in different groups. Their varying lifestyles resulted in differences in the mental makeups of the tribal belonging to different groups. Likewise their concept of problems, joys and sorrows, financial conditions, their ailments, their hopes and aspirations, their yearnings for living life differed substantially. Hence their habits of drinking varied too; and so did their reasons for drinking.

Tribal are not aware of hazardous effects of drinking. It is the need of time to make awareness in tribal society for these abuses. Every day we can see tribal use to drink heavily. If there is any family function or small ceremony then there is none of other way than drinking alcohol to celebrate. It is very dangerous even to drink heavily on a single occasion too. I have discussed this issue in detail in my thesis. That can prove as eye opener to all.

So far brain is concerned, alcohol causes problems in the brain's communication system and can affect the way the brain looks and works. This may effect mood and behaviour and deteriorate thinking capacity. After a heavy drink at night you will realize feeling dizzy and your head hurts. You might not remember everything you did the previous night. One can easily realize how quickly and dramatically alcohol affects the brain. There are long lasting consequences of alcohol consumption on the brain.

Another important organ is liver. Uncontrolled drinking can lead to various liver problems like Alcoholic hepatitis, Fibrosis and Cirrhosis. While our liver works hard to keep the body productive and healthy, it also stores energy and nutrients. It also generates proteins and enzymes to ward off disease. The liver breaks down most of the alcohol a person consumes. But in the process of breaking alcohol, it generates toxins which are more harmful than alcohol itself. These toxins damage liver cells, promote inflammation, and weaken the body's natural defence. These problems disrupt the metabolism of the body and disrupt function of other organs. Since, the liver plays such a vital role in alcohol detoxification, excessive alcohol severely damage the liver. Fatty liver; the condition called as steatosis is the earliest stage of alcoholic liver disease which makes it more difficult for the liver to operate properly. Several complications, including jaundice, insulin resistance, diabetes and even liver cancer, can result as cirrhosis weakens liver function. Alcohol alters the chemicals in the liver needed to break down and remove this scar tissue. As a result, liver function suffers. If one continues to drink, this excessive scar tissue builds up and creates a condition called cirrhosis, which is a slow deterioration of the liver.

The problems related to health of heart are very dangerous. Heavy drink over a long time can damage the heart may cause problems of irregular heart beat known as Arrhythmias, cardiomyopathy, High blood pressure, etc. However, limited consumption of alcohol may prevent heart disease. But when villagers drink they don't know any limitations. Alcoholic cardiomyopathy is a condition due to weakness to heart muscles caused by daily heavy drinking habits. As a result, the enough blood cannot be pumped up to the organs which may severe damage to organs and tissues. Problems of shortness of breath, fatigue, swollen legs and feet, and irregular heartbeat, and other breathing complications can be noticed in alcoholic cardiomyopathy.

Heavy drinking habit is at the risk of developing cancer of mouth, throat, breast and liver. Drinking too much also leads to weaken immune system. Diseases like Pneumonia and tuberculosis are also found developed in chronic drinkers. Daily drinking slows your body's ability to ward off infections.

Pancreas is the most important organ in our digestion system. Toxic substances are produced in pancreas that may lead to pancreatitis, a dangerous inflammation and swelling of the blood vessels in the pancreas that prevents proper digestion. The pancreas plays an important role in food digestion and its conversion into fuel to power your body. It sends enzymes into the small intestine to digest carbohydrates, proteins, and fat. It also secretes insulin and glucagon. Insulin also ensures that extra glucose gets stored away as either glycogen or fat. When a person drinks, alcohol damages pancreatic cells and disrupts metabolic processes. This process leaves the pancreas open to dangerous inflammations. Abdominal pain, vomiting, Fever, Rapid heart rate, Diarrhoea, and Sweating are the symptoms of an acute pancreatic attack.

Cancer Risks cannot be underestimated. It cannot be said about the genetically transferred diseases. But the environment and lifestyle habits can be responsible for getting chronic diseases like cancer, tuberculosis, asthma, etc. We are unable to do anything to change our genes, and we cannot change our environment too. We can definitely make some changes in our lifestyle habits if those are hazardous to our living. The studies identify consumption of alcohol may affect you with following types of cancer: Mouth, Liver, Breast, Larynx and throat.

Too much consumption of alcohol can be dangerous to our life and it can be to the extent of disease like cancer. This does not mean that anyone who drinks too much will develop cancer. But going through medical and scientific data available; shows the increased possibility of certain types of cancer.

The work concerning studying the tribal way of life, arranging group discussions, counselling, etc. though very arduous, was quite fascinating too. Like a scientist I was making new discoveries every day. Listening to the many stories concerning tribal gave me goose pimples. Drinking for them had become a necessity of life and many of the tribal considered it as absolutely natural. It was necessary to make them aware about the grave implications of consuming alcohol, the deterioration of the natural physical strength. There were many charitable NGOs and government institutions that work in the field of tribal welfare. This was a time consuming job. In the course of our project study we realised that the NGOs and the government institutions were not able to achieve the desired success in the programs for eradication of alcoholism due to various problems like limitations in the mental abilities of the tribal in understanding the advice against drinking, inadequate education facilities, unorganised and slow rate of rural development, inability of the facilities under the government schemes in reaching the rural tribal areas and apathy shown by the government staff.

Dr. APJ Kalam continued, 'my message to you, young friends, is that: education gives you wings to fly. Achievements come out of the fire in our subconscious mind that 'I will win'. So each one of you assembled here and elsewhere, will have 'wings of fire'. The wings of fire will indeed lead to knowledge which will make you fly as a doctor, or an engineer or a scientist or a teacher or a political leader or a bureaucrat or a diplomat or anything that you want to be.'

Amongst all I truly appreciated Dr Kalam's speech. In his characteristic simple style he addressed the necessity of focussing on issues like significance of education, the challenges before the University to keep up with the modern trends, the changes to be anticipated and ways to develop the ability to take decisions in students while working in a team.

This was followed by the program of conferring the degrees. At the outset the famous scientist, Dr Shri Vijay Bhatkar was conferred the highest award of the D Lit degree. Dr Bhatkar is a world renowned scientist having invented the Param supercomputer. He hailed from Nagpur and all of us at Nagpur were very proud of this honour bestowed upon him. This was followed the PhD awarding ceremony for the one thousand students. This for me was the most important part of today's program. Names were being called out and one by one the names from the sound systems were falling on my ears. It was the height of excitement and expectancy. I was in a state of trance. There were no thoughts; only a wait to hear my name being announced. On hearing my name I just had to walk up to the stage – that's all that was there in my mind.

And finally the name was announced! 'Ms Kama Naitam, PhD, and the subject of my PhD ......'I left my seat immediately and walked quietly up to the stage and touched Dr Kalam's feet respectfully. My name and the subject of my thesis were announced once again. Dr Kalam handed over my degree to me and shook my hand smilingly. Someone handed over a medal in an envelope to Dr Kalam and he himself put the medal around my neck and congratulated me. Dr Kalam was such a great scientist and today I was standing there, right in front of him! Such a well-known personality but from close quarters his face looked so unaffected and it carried such an easy smile! His body language implied that he entertained no false notions about his greatness. Such people are so simple; is that the reason they achieve so much greatness? I felt like talking to him at length but this was neither the place nor the time. But it was also true that there will never be another chance. The eyes of the people on the dais as well as of those sitting in the front rows were focussed on me. I bowed and greeted those on the dais as well as those in the audience, and once again paid my respects to Dr Kalam and then climbed down the steps at the side of the stage. As directed earlier I had to remain seated till the end of the program. So I came and sat down in my seat. I was as happy as ever but now I was completely at peace. My dream had been fulfilled and my efforts had paid off. My efforts had borne fruit. I had crossed a landmark in my life. I had reached one of my destinations.

The convocation centenary celebrations were now at an end. The dignitaries on the dais and all those present in the *shamiyana* who had got on their feet for the national anthem, had started to disperse.

While I was leaving I noticed my guide, Dr Gade coming towards me. 'Congratulations, Dr Naitam!,' he exclaimed. Shaking my hand he gave a cheerful smile.

I replied, 'Thank you very much, Sir' and bowed to him.

After speaking with me for a couple of minutes Dr Gade casually invited me over to his place and then got busy with the others beside him.

Until now I had not seen Guruji. I started towards the *shamiyana* entrance to look for him. I was anxious to meet the divine personality whose profound blessings and relentless efforts had made this day a reality. I was restless to meet this great personality. It was his inspiration that made me to work hard for PhD. Left to me my PhD would have remained just a dream. Since the last some years Guruji had done the invaluable work of turning that dream into reality. All his divine powers had been channelized into making me complete my PhD. This ordinary looking person had been enlightened with *Hanumant* powers. Hanumant himself was living through him. I was just instrumental in the PhD. All the hard work, field work was done by Guruji. The PhD was rightfully his; and I wanted to offer it to him. Whilst walking, I noticed Guruji sitting in the front row and apparently he was looking around for me. I could see clearly in his expression how anxious he was to find me.

Tears gave way as I bent down to touch Guruji's feet. Guruji drew me up and moved his hand over my head. There was ecstasy in Guruji's face and his eyes shone with tears. I don't know whether he congratulated me, but he uttered something with quivering lips. Overwhelmed with happiness, maybe he was at a loss for words. My tears of joy accepted the congratulations from the teary eyes and unsteady lips. I could sense the sentiments in those quivering whispers uttered by Guruji. This moment lapped up the emotions that were by far more expressive and unbarred by formalities stuck in the cobwebs of words like 'congratulations' and 'thank you'. During the period I was preparing for my PhD, I had the privilege of experiencing the power that existed in the blessings of an enlightened, divine soul. Right from day one of my PhD project until its completion I had felt the repercussions of Guruji's power. Right from the start I had never looked back. Every moment of my PhD work was supported by Guruji's virtual presence in the form of his divine power. Whenever I made a mention about this divine power Guruji would divert all the credit to Hanumanji and would say that it was blessings of Hanumanji that enables us to perform big tasks. He would quickly recite *Jal Dhi Langhi Gaye Achraj Nahi*; *meaning: no surprise if one crosses the Ocean* at such times. (Lines from *Hanuman Chalisa*)

With teary eyes Guruji looked at the medal put on me by Dr Kalam. He touched it to his forehead in a manner of thanks giving. Immense satisfaction reflected in his face. He indicated at the vacant chair next to him for me to sit. Both of us were sitting. Just then my brother, sister-in-law and my son, Shyam, came looking for me. Brother and sister-in-law paid their obeisance to Guruji.

'Congratulations, Dr Kama,' they exclaimed happily. And my brother had embraced me. Sister-in-law, too, held me in her arms. Shyam too came and hugged me. Guruji was talking to my son and said something about a grand celebration; and both of them burst out laughing.

There are many highly qualified people in the world with PhDs and there number is on the rise. So what's the big deal? That's what most people must be thinking. But for me it was a major achievement, a big success, in my life. Until now I had lived a life full of adversities, and therefore I never entertained any hopes that anything would ever be achieved by me. Success was a distant matter; even a few happy moments in my life were hard to come by. Every phase was a struggle. There was humiliation to be borne at every important juncture. My entire life was overcome with depression. I abused my own reflection in the mirror. ' What you are a wretched creature! Why the hell were you born at all?' I would ask myself loathingly and walk away. The constant flow of misery refused to allow any trace of excitement in my life. I carried the baggage of humiliations and frustrations with me that turned me into a living corpse. With no will power, no confidence, no optimism, my life was like a vehicle without fuel being thrust forward, dragging towards nowhere.

With life passing through such gruelling circumstances when at last I found my way out and eventually managed to get the PhD, it was indeed a spectacular event in my life. This would not have been possible without the presence of a divine influence in my life.

My Love

Just the two of us, Siddharth and I, were sitting on the bank of the river *Wainganga*. Whenever time permitted, once in a week or a fortnight, he would take his car out. For a change I too looked forward to spending time in those peaceful surroundings. Various subjects would be discussed. I would share my problems with him. He too was an empathetic listener and would be truly saddened on hearing about my past adversities. My Siddharth was very sensitive.

Wainganga was a huge expanse of a river. It flowed down the left from somewhere in Madhya Pradesh and here the riverbed had turned very deep and wide as well. *Wainganga* is a river of India, which originates about twelve Kilomtres from Mundara village of Seoni district in the southern slopes of the Satpura Range of Madhya Pradesh, and flows towards south through Madhya Pradesh and Maharashtra. Towards the left it appeared to flow in a curve amidst the forest greenery and remained full round the year. On the right it flowed on and on in a straight line as far as the eyes could see, disappearing into the horizon. There was a mountain far across, momentarily appearing as though it was blocking the river flow. This river was supposed to be passing through our tribal province and flowing towards Andhra Pradesh.

What a vast distance a river has to travel, I wondered. Finding its way through so many difficult twists and turns, cutting across jungles, mountains and valleys on the way, it continues resolutely with its journey towards the far away horizon. Struggling through the various conditions, it takes into its fold the many troubles and hardships on the way and absorbs them into the deep riverbed. And still on the face of it the flow of the river appears so exuberant, joyful and attractive! In our country the rivers enjoy a very sacred status.

Rivers are addressed as mother. While In the north the Ganges is called *Ganga ma*, this is our own *Wainganga Maa* (*The mother*). I think the river is revered like a mother may be for this reason. We regard our mother as our first teacher. It is by holding our mother's finger that we take our first steps in life. That is our first guru in the form of our mother who shows us the way in our childhood, teaches us to walk on the path of life. A river's eternal, ceaseless journey is full of adversities and challenges just like that of human life. Many definitions of human life are created in the process of this journey. Hence river means to be continuously on the move. No matter what the weather, be it summer, winter or the rains, it continues to flow ceaselessly while struggling with the onslaught of adverse circumstances. Sitting on the bank and watching the deep wide expanse of the river for hours on end is one of my favourite pastimes. In the evening the colourful hues emerging from the skies reach out to their reflections in the water. Every colour, every shade flaunts its distinctive nature, and along with the changing shades of the skies reflects the corresponding shades, appearing as though divine rays were being transmitted from somewhere in the depths of the waters. May be that is why the various waves of emotions come gushing to the mind creating a divine exuberance. The glow in the depths of the water appears like a vibrant halo around an enlightened soul. Was the extremely exotic and amazing scenario experienced only by us or was it a common feature open to all?

The evening had elapsed and in the intermediary twilight phase the water acquired a deeper shade, lending sombreness to the ambience. My mind that was so joyous a while ago had once again acquired seriousness like the water below. The ripples in the water aroused parallel sensations in the mind. The evening was getting increasingly dark. While the depth of the water was a measurable entity, the depth of the mind was unfathomable. The thoughts went on and on. There was no end to the innumerable thoughts being churned out and I was totally submerged in the recesses of my mind.

Siddharth asked, 'Kama, what's the matter, what's going on?' But I was in my own world and did not hear.

'Kama, where are you lost?' Siddharth enquired once again, holding my hand. 'What are you thinking so much about?'

I gasped at being awakened from my reverie and looked at Siddharth. Amazed, he was trying to look searchingly into my eyes. But in the pitch darkness he kept on staring as if trying to catch a glimpse of the moon hidden behind the clouds.

'Can you see the various shades of colours inside the deep waters?' I asked.

'Of course,' Siddharth replied.

I continued, 'I was preoccupied in observing those various changing shades; so much so that I discerned a link between the natural flow of the river and our human way of life'.

Siddharth commented, 'Hope you're not getting serious again!'

"No Siddhu, I am not serious. In fact I think I have discovered a new dimension of life. "I answered.

Life is like that.... There are so many hurdles, so many twists and turns in our lives. God makes us undergo so many adversities. So often we lose heart and tend to give up in difficult situations and feel unhappy. Sometimes we just get stuck. We lose patience, we get into depression. But truly, as written in our religious texts, river is like our mother. Just as a mother shows us the right way and is our first teacher, similarly there is a lot that we can learn from the river. Our life should take lessons from a river to remain pure and clean. The river constantly flows over so many different places, drawing the waste away from village after village. But you will notice it does not accumulate any of the dirt within itself. Disposing the dirt of on the shores, it makes its way ahead and lives up to its status as pure and clean. No wonder our ancient scriptures refer to it with so much reverence.

We too should traverse our future path bravely and joyfully without losing courage due to the sweet and sour experiences in life. Today, sitting on the river bank I am going through an extraordinary feeling of happiness. I am rejuvenated and feeling refreshed as if a riddle of life has been sorted out. The myriad questions bothering my mind have been answered. Mental lethargy has been washed away by the waters and my mind feels absolutely pure and clean.

Siddharth and I came to know each during our daily travel by train. Siddharth was a Class I officer in the government service in the same town where I was employed. Handsome, tall and with a solemn but calm expression, he was apparently my age or may be a little older. He was mostly seen wearing glares. I had never seen him whiling away amidst a crowd or at the tea stall. He would occupy just about any vacant seat in the train. He was reserved and would often be seen immersed in a book in the train. Sometimes during our way home when the train was late by a couple of hours, the other department employees would be seen chitchatting, playing cards or indulging in pranks at the platform; but he would be engrossed in a book. It is hilarious the way we came to know each other. In fact our friendship started after a minor squabble.

One day on my way home the train was very late. At such times I generally got extremely tired and became impatient for the train to arrive and find a seat to settle down. I suppose the menfolk felt the same way too. At last the train arrived. The halt was just for two minutes and there was a mad rush at the entrance. The men naturally got in first and grabbed seats for themselves. When I got in with my friends there was a clamour for seats. I looked around and saw Siddharth and the other men sitting comfortably on the benches. But there was no place left for me and my friends. My friends were all grumbling away and in the midst of all that chaos this person was sitting peacefully with his head buried in a book. And that's not all! He looked up from his book and had the audacity to say, 'Madam, please be quiet. What's the point in yelling? 'And so on. As it is I was dead tired and exasperated waiting for the train for so long. I lost my patience and started lashing out at the entire male species. They were useless, devoid of any manners, considered themselves educated but didn't have the basic courtesy to offer seats to ladies, and so on. Perhaps like us the delay by the train had exasperated Siddharth too. He too couldn't take my outburst any more. My friends also had spoken a bit too much. For one, Siddharth had just been transferred and was new here, while ours was an old group. There was a major altercation and I had already blurted out more than was necessary. And that was it. He got up from his seat and walked away abruptly. He had been badly insulted by me and my friends. For the time being it was a winning moment for us in the ladies group. The group was pleased with my initiative. But he was mortified being the brunt of our insults in full view of the other passengers. We were all in a self-congratulatory mode at the thought of having had our way with the menfolk and went home elated.

Siddharth was a Class I officer in government service. He was not frivolous like the others and we knew that. During the argument he had not once lost control over his words and his language itself bespoke of his cultured antecedents.

For quite some time after the said incident Siddharth was not to be seen either on the railway station or during the journey. We went to work and commuted by train as usual. He had almost disappeared for around fifteen-twenty days. Questions arose in my mind. I should not have insulted a decent person like him on such a trivial issue. It was really wrong on my part; the regret kept gnawing at me every day. Squabbles with fellow passengers were a part of train travel and I had never given it much thought. This incident however made me feel very uneasy. Though such incidents happen, women do harbour a fear that if we offend the menfolk during the journey they might get back at us at some later time. But in this case what happened was quite unexpected. The person simply vanished from the scene.

I started getting increasingly restless and was overridden by a sense of guilt. I yearned to meet him and apologise. Will he speak to me, or will he take me to be just another woman, I wondered. Various doubts engulfed my mind. Why I was being so sympathetic towards this stranger was something I could not fathom. I knew my nature; I was not at all sensitive and generally would not allow myself to get carried away by such an incident.

Our train was scheduled for 9:10, morning. But today it was late by thirty minutes. Whether on time or late, I was invariably rushed. When it was on time I would reach just when the train was about to start and when it was late, it was the same case. I would hear the whistle of the guard just as I reached the platform, as if he was waiting for me to come!

After a good night's sleep I was feeling so pleasant and refreshed in the morning. Outside on starting the scooter the cold breeze flowing against the body felt delightful. Moreover the warm rays of the sun were gratifying too. Today it seemed as though the sun had risen especially for me and so had the flow of the breeze. Isn't the human mind astounding! A happy consciousness has the power to bring about a change in the entire universe. The waves of happiness emanating from the consciousness appeared to be competing with the rays of the sun outside. My heart was that of an innocent child, free of all conflict!

The branches and the flowers in the garden were swaying along with the breeze and my tranquil mind too was swaying on the rhythm of the breeze flowing softly against my body as I rode the scooter. I was savouring every moment!

After parking my scooter at the stand outside the railway station I rushed towards the platform. And it was the same scenario as usual! The guard, as if waiting for me, gave a long whistle and waved out his green flag. I quickly entered a compartment and no sooner I found a seat, I was in for a shock! Siddharth was sitting right there on the seat opposite mine. Amidst the hustle and bustle of passengers he sat there as usual reading a book with a serene expression on his face. It felt nice seeing him this way. Almost three weeks had passed since the last incident in the train. I had fully ascertained the repercussions of my outburst and was restless ever since that day. I felt guilty, and moreover, this person had disappeared from the scene altogether, making me all the more curious about him. I had all along hoped to meet him some day and convey my apology.

However, Siddharth was engrossed in his book and not the least bothered about his co-passengers. I had come and sat there right in front of him but he hardly noticed me. He had no inkling of the turmoil in my mind. For a moment a thought flashed in my mind. I wondered if it was really necessary for me to apologise. Why should I lower myself? May be that was my ego coming in the way. The train had picked up speed. On looking through the window the far away trees appeared to be rushing towards the train and the closer ones were moving away backwards at the same speed. For a while I was absorbed in watching the trees. I imagined the trees spaced out in the form of a circle outside the train. The closer ones appeared to move backwards tracing a huge circular path and moving forward once again appearing in the front.

In my mind I too was churning the same thoughts. I had accepted the fact that I was wrong. And that was the reason I genuinely wanted to apologise. The train halted momentarily and so did the far away trees that were marching forward in a circle in an orderly manner. For a moment my urge to apologise was overshadowed by my egoistic thoughts. But like the good overpowering the evil, I decided to go by my nobler instinct. I owed it to myself that I apologise. It was necessary for my mental well-being. That would relieve me of my guilt. In fact in doing so I would be forgiving myself. From the time we make a mistake till the time we apologise and further till we are forgiven for it, for the entire period we continuously inflict abuse on ourselves. I consider it a form of violence on our own self. This has an adverse effect on the sanctity of our mind. And moreover it is we ourselves that are responsible for the violence. If we do not attend to this in time, there is a possibility of its causing permanent damage to our pure and clean mind by turning it cruel and shameless.

I finally decided to interrupt Siddharth. ' Good morning! Sir' Siddharth jerked his head from his book and looked at me with a faint smile.

'Good morning, Madam. Good morning!' he replied, giving the impression that nothing in particular had happened between us and that he had moved on after the incident.

Before he could resume reading I said, 'Sorry to disturb you but I want to speak to you.'

Siddharth looked at me with expressionless face. 'Yes?'

I began, 'Sir, I'm extremely sorry for the way I behaved the other day. Please forgive me.'

Like a cool breeze from a fleeting shadow spread by the unexpected cloudy skies amidst scorching heat, Siddharth's normal solemn expression gave way to a hearty laughter. 'Oh, the hot argument! that day?' He had apparently forgotten about the incident.

'Madam, why are you making such an issue of it?"

And once again trying to recall the incident he continue 'Madam, actually I should have been the one to apologise. It was my mistake. I'm really sorry'.

Siddharth was a thorough gentleman and had displayed chivalry befitting a Class-I officer. I found this attitude most praiseworthy. I sensed the presence of a soft and pure heart behind the façade of a solemn and severe exterior. Such incidents convince us that one cannot judge a person merely by his face. So often we ascertain the nature of a person based on his facial expressions giving rise to so many biases, favourable or otherwise, and then decide upon the behaviour to be meted out to him. That's absolutely wrong.

I was thoroughly pleased. I felt like a prisoner being honourably and unconditionally released. I myself had set my mind free with my self-respect intact. By asking for forgiveness we ourselves get our minds cleansed and we can actually feel the purity. This was one of the rare occasions in life when I was truly happy. I was completely relaxed. In life there are many occasions that bring us joy. We can share this happiness with others which in turn reflects in our face. By narrating about our happy events to others we are able to cheer them up too. One cannot feel the importance of this intrinsic happiness without actually going through the experience. Asking for forgiveness for one's wrong doing is one such activity that brings us phenomenal happiness. One should get down to doing it and experience the unique happiness for oneself.

As it is my day had started on a very cheerful note. Right from the flowing breeze to the cool sun rays, all had contributed to my day today. It is said that the day that starts well, goes well. Thus today had started with happiness and exuberance, and put me on the top of the world!

The train was in full speed. The station was expected in about five to ten minutes. Apart from the routine travellers the other commuters were struggling to get hold of their baggage from under the nearby seats before getting down. By now I had got used to the daily commuting, different types of commuters every day, their various discussions, political discussions, minor arguments, haggling with vendors, etc. So I did not take anything too seriously. Sometimes even the vendors become familiar. They help in making way through the crowds and finding seats. The ticket checking staff also becomes familiar to the daily commuters. Those who travel to and fro on a daily basis are a class by themselves. Many of them do not know one another by names, nor do they speak to one another but they all know one another by face. Such daily commuters are like one big family. Sometimes we see someone's birthday being celebrated. A cake is cut and there is a small party in the train itself. One can see the essence of life being played out in that 1 to 1½ hours' journey. For people like us who commute on a daily basis the major part of their lives is spent in train travel. I have many a times seen pujas being performed during festival *Dussera* or prayers being offered to the idol of Goddess *Lakshmi* in the

---

Dussera – A festival is celebrated in India after Nine Holy days of Durga Puja. The day also marks the victory of Goddess Durga over the demon Mahisasura.

Laxmi – Goddesss Laxmi. Diety of wealth. According to Hindu Mythology wife of Lord Vishnu.

evenings during *Diwali*. Thus the regular commuters make the most of their rail journey and treat it as an occasion to celebrate life.

The daily commuters tend to nurture a bond amongst them. All of them lend a helping hand to one another and share good and bad happenings in their lives. However, when someone gets transferred to some other place then he has to leave the group and go away. For a while he is missed. Similarly, when a new person is transferred here, he soon gets absorbed in the group and becomes a part of it. When a person appears bored during the to and fro journey, it is easy to identify him as a new entrant. Siddharth belonged to this category. He had recently been transferred and was now among the daily commuters. I had come to know him through this episode of my offering apology. A new personality, a thorough gentleman, had now subscribed to the family of the regular commuters.

I asked, 'Do you keep reading all the time? You seem to be a voracious reader!'

Siddharth replied, 'I am very fond of reading; right from the beginning.'

He did not seem to be too enthusiastic about replying or conversing with me and was back to reading.

'Sir, what book are you reading?' I asked simply, as it was not possible to see the name on the front page as the book was covered by a newspaper. The next station was expected to arrive at any moment now.

Diwali-A Great Hindu festival in India worshipping Goddess Laxmi & Goddess Kali. Diwali means rows of lighted lamps. It is a festival of lights, and all Indian celebrate it joyfully. In this festival, people light up their houses and shops

Siddharth shut the book and started shoving it into his bag. "I got hold of this excellent book on the subject of The Guiding Principles of Gautam Buddha. It's very interesting."

By then the train had come to a standstill at the station. We said our good-byes and that was the end of our morning journey.

Asking for forgiveness means the action of expressing my sincere regret as performed by me when I have made a mistake because of which someone has suffered. Nobody likes the complicated, defeated feelings and to admit his own mistake. Admitting one's mistake is considered some kind of a defeat. No one is prepared to say 'I am wrong' either in public or in private. Everyone considers it humiliating and as lowering oneself. It hurts the ego. It is, literally, humiliating, since apologizing almost always requires humility and a willingness to put the needs of those you have wronged over your own. For ego-bound creatures and we are all ego-bound, this is a hard thing to do.

Then why apologise at all? The Greek word *apologia* means a defence or justification, offering defensive arguments, making excuses. An apology is an admission that you've wronged others and that you are actually sorry for it. The reason to apologize is not because other people expect it from you, but because you expect it from yourself — it is part of your personal character to own up to the wrongs you have done to others. How important is asking for forgiveness? Firstly it expresses your sorrow for having committed the act and it is also a sincere admission of the fact that you have harmed the other person. One should also remember that asking for forgiveness is not admission of guilt. An apology is not a confession. You can confess your faults to anyone who is prepared to listen, but you can apologize only to the one you have harmed.

After all we are all human beings and it is not necessary that we should be perfect in all respects all the time. It is true that some time or the other everyone makes a mistake and then apology is the only option. Else, if you are so confident of yourself and want to pamper your ego, in that case you should never make any mistake at all. In fact apologising is not for cowards at all. To admit one's mistakes and ask for forgiveness requires a big heart. It requires a lot of courage. An apology involves acknowledging that a wrong has been done.

There should be no problem is apologising when we have wronged someone. For one, by rendering an apology we get to interact with the offended person. The fact that we are accepting our mistake gives a sense of satisfaction to the other person and he too gets a chance to interact with us. When you offer an apology you certify yourself as having done wrong. And this admission itself creates a trust that once again facilitates in normalising your relationship. Besides this when we accept all our mistakes we also generate due respect for the harmed person. When we accept complete responsibility for our mistakes, for something going wrong, it adds to our own confidence, self-respect and dignity.

Moving from making apologies to receiving them, the response to an apology is acceptance, not forgiveness. Forgiveness and accepting an apology are very close, but with some differences. One can forgive someone even if not asked for apology.

Jesus's prayer was for his executioners. Father, forgive them; they know not what they do. Christ forgave his executioners. Forgiveness and accepting an apology are two different issues. Forgiveness can be a part of authority; however making apology is a noble thought has to be aroused from within.

What started as an apology led to a lasting friendship between Siddharth and me. He thought of me with respect and considered me to be cultured, educated and someone with an idealistic approach to life. He would always speak to me sparingly and to the point but was very articulate as well. I found him very respectful when interacting with me. Whenever he spoke, I just wanted him to go on and on, and it was a pleasure to hear him speak.

Today Siddharth was with me but was not carrying any book.

'Sir, the other day in the train you were so engrossed in a book. What was so special about it?' I asked, before he could take out a book from his bag.

Siddharth replied, 'That was a very interesting book. I could grasp the entire philosophy of Buddhist religion from it.'

'Still, could you explain in short?' I asked.

I did not turn out short at all. Siddharth spoke continuously for almost an hour about the Buddhist religion. Whatever the religion, all of them teach us how human life can be lived with happiness, peace and harmony. Gautam Buddha founded the Buddhist religion. The religion has been named after him. By coincidence Gautam Buddha's name was also Siddharth like mine. This Siddharth later on became Siddharth Gautam Buddha. The religion originated in India in the 6th century B.C. Siddharth was born in a Hindu royal family. The unbearable sorrows, pains of human life in the world had a profound impact on the young and sensitive Siddharth and raised many questions in his mind. He gave up his kingdom and all the comforts that go with it, as also his home and family, and set out to discover the mysteries of human life. For many years he travelled far and wide, wandering through jungles, cities and wildernesses, doing severe penance bearing the substance of his ultimate goal in mind. And finally one day he attained enlightenment.

The following are the tenets of Buddhism:

1. Sacrifice of livings beings, idol worship are meaningless rituals.
2. Good character, good behaviour propagates good things and bad character, bad behaviour results in misery.
3. The creator did not create the caste system enforced by Hindu clerics.
4. One who attains full wisdom is entitled to salvation and becomes free of the unending chain of life and death.
5. The world was always in existence and will continue to exist till eternity.
6. The ultimate aim of life should not be merely to find happiness or enjoyment of physical comforts but to eliminate sorrow from life.

Buddhism propagates many such beliefs and put forward four noble truths before the world. Accordingly amongst the many causes of sorrow in life the main ones are old age, sickness, death, failure and separation. The urge to gratify desires/expectations forms an important part of human life. Control or diminution of these desires/expectations is necessary to relieve oneself of the sorrows in life.

Although I am Hindu by birth, I valued these teachings of the Buddhist religion which are very appropriate for making human life happy, peaceful and harmonious, and should be inculcated. Buddhism is also found to highlight the importance of meditation, having introduced the practice of *Vipaschyana* which is popular worldwide.

Such meetings with Siddharth involved exchange of ideas on a wide range of subjects. Hindu religion was also a subject of our discussions. Like in Buddhism, Hindu philosophy propagated the law of karma, or the fruits of our actions. According to this we have to face the repercussions of every action of ours. Good actions beget joy and bad actions beget sorrow. Various religions of the world featured in our discussions. The end of every discussion made us realise that practically every religion propagated the same teachings that were aimed at improving the quality of human life. Whatever differences we notice on certain issues are the propagated by the so called religious scholars. At the end of the day I feel human religion is the most important of all religions. From every religious scripture one should inculcate the principles that contribute towards betterment of human life. Every person should be accorded human treatment. It is improper to expose anyone to injustice or harassment. No one should be subjected to exploitation. One by one the lives of the entire human race should be made happy. If the new

---

Vipaschyana – Vipaschyana meditation is an ancient practice taught by Buddhas

generation follows this rule the human life will be benefitted and the human religion will be practised.

Since childhood I had been brought up in the culture of the eternal Hindu religion. Idol worship was followed at home and so I did it too. But I was open to adapting good from any religion. It is my firm belief that principles of any religion are formulated with the intention of brining happiness to human life. Therefore if we study in depth the teachings and literatures of religious preceptors we will definitely notice a similarity in their thoughts expressed in them. As mentioned earlier, Buddhism teachings propagate that good results from good culture, good behaviour and vice versa. The law of karma in Hinduism says the same. Whatever good or bad deeds we do, the result will be correspondingly good or bad. As per the laws of physics, every action has an equal and opposite reaction. It is true that every good or bad deed of ours is followed by good or bad result in the corresponding proportion.

Siddharth was a voracious reader and had in-depth knowledge in any subject of discussion. There was lot to be learnt from discussions with him.

Today on my way home on reaching the station I came to know that the train was late by forty minutes. Generally people called up the station beforehand to know about the train timings. I, however, came straight to the station after finishing my work. Resting myself on a bench I started studying for my MPSC exams. As recommended by Siddharth I had applied for the Class I Government officer's post. The exam was due in twenty- twenty five days and it was necessary to study as and when I found time. As the train was late by forty minutes, the time was up by now and most of the regular commuters from all offices had arrived at the station. Though I was studying, my attention was in between distracted by people passing by me. Siddharth had not reached the station as yet. I didn't know why but I would get restless if I did not see Siddharth. If this train was missed the next one was due after full three hours. That is why everyone was so determined to catch this particular train. Continuous announcements were being made on the public address system about the arrival of the train. I shut my book and kept a watch on the route leading to the platform and waited impatiently for Siddharth to come. It's not as if I spoke to Siddharth every day; he too would just smile at me, and that's about all! But just his presence at the station and in the train was something that made me feel very nice. It was very reassuring. If he was not there I missed him terribly. His absence made me very restless.

The train was now at the platform but there was no sign of Siddharth as yet. In order that I did not miss him I deliberately walked towards the end of the train and got into the compartment next to that of the guard's cabin. After waiting for a couple of minutes the guard blew the whistle and the train started moving. I was continuously looking out from the window. If Siddharth turned up now he could still make it. I wished Siddharth would come soon even if the train had to delay by another couple of minutes. I fervently prayed Siddharth should catch this train and looked anxiously out of the window for him. The train started slowly but was gradually picking up speed. At that moment I suddenly noticed Siddharth running with his bag behind the train. I was waving out to him signalling him to run and catch the train but perhaps he did not see me. Siddharth was running continuously but the train was now in good speed and I realised it was not possible for him to make it to the train. Siddharth appeared exhausted after the long run. He was on the platform just about fifty feet behind the train but now he had given up and stopped running as the train was in full speed. Gradually he was out of sight. I felt disappointed that God did not listen to my sincere prayers. Siddharth had missed the train just by a couple of minutes.

In fact missing a train was no big deal for the daily commuters. Every now and then someone or the other for whatever reason missed the train. Now almost half-an-hour had passed since the train started but I was still in a restless frame of mind. Siddharth in a blue shirt running behind the train and then giving up the chase in disappointment, continued to come before my eyes. His missing the train had really saddened me.

Why did I get so upset for Siddharth? Why did I feel elated when I saw him? Why was I upset by his absence? What magic did his personality hold for me? I derived great pleasure from communicating with him and yearned to meet him again and again. Was I in love with him? How one could fall in love at my age was an insoluble riddle for me.

I was now married for thirteen years. I had a twelve years old son. That I could still fall for someone at this stage was a surprise for my own self. Nevertheless the fact of the matter is that until now I had never ever fallen in love with anyone. Yes, I was married. It is also true that I had a son born through my physical union with a man who was no better than a wild beast. But there had not been an iota of love in my destiny. The relationship that I shared with my husband was that of a machine that satisfied his lust. The marriage arranged by my people had proved to be a curse for me. My mother had got me married but I never experienced what a man's love meant.

Oh, those six months in the company of that wild male! Marriage is supposed to be a sacred relationship, the beginning of life long journey of a promising companionship. But in my case, marriage turned out to be a blemish on my life that could never be erased. It drove me to develop a loathing for the entire male species. I started believing that men messed up this pure and auspicious relationship and made it so complicated and foul. No sooner had I finished my education I was married off and then my son was born. I returned to my maternal home on the pretext of taking rest, never to go back again, and thus managed to escape from the clutches of that beast of a husband. I simply refused to return to that hell again.

During my college days I was fully into my studies. After marriage I had given myself up to satisfy my husband's carnal needs. With the birth of my son came the responsibility of motherhood. As my son grew up I took over the responsibility as her guardian. And then there was the question of earning a livelihood. Complications from every angle threw my life in a state of despair. Life was starved of the tenderness of love. Stories of love and romance that I had read in books appeared so shallow. Plastic flowers looked beautiful in a bouquet and I believed love too was false and lifeless like those plastic flowers and looked attractive only in stories and novels.

And now here I was in love with Siddharth! Day and night he occupied my mind, my thoughts. Every memory of his was a source of joy to me. Just a glimpse of him at the station or in the train would make my day. His personality, the smile that escaped his lips betraying his solemn expression, looked so painfully attractive. His reticence, his loneliness, disciplined life-style and orderliness was drawing me towards him.

I would go out of my way to create excuses to meet him. As it was not possible to talk freely at the station or in the train we would generally decide upon some beautiful natural surroundings to meet up. Once in a week or a fortnight we would meet at a quiet place and hold discussions on various subjects for hours together.

Siddharth was older to me and was married. I had disclosed to him all about my past life and he treated me sympathetically. I was aware that I had a 12 year old son and that I was no longer a carefree youngster. But once bitten twice shy, and I had decided to take care and tread on safe grounds this time around.

I liked Siddharth immensely and loved him from my heart. But these were my feelings and I had decided to keep them to myself. In this shattered life of mine I was not taking any more chances. Although deeply in love I never revealed my feelings to Siddharth. I thoroughly enjoyed his company and the discussions that we had together. He was very well read and his in-depth knowledge in various subjects was a great boost to my knowledge. Siddharth was very restrained and hailed from a good respectable family. He was a responsible officer. He used to behave with me with utmost respect and compassion, offer me companionship and overall we enjoyed a very good rapport. His feelings towards me, if he nurtured any love for me or not, did not figure in our conversation. However, one must admit that people of opposite sex do get attracted at some point in time. And moreover if their thoughts, behaviour and temperaments are compatible, a strong bond of friendship becomes possible. That is when it becomes possible to spend long hours together. Deep friendship is not feasible without attraction. Eventually how this friendship takes the form of love, or in fact how to proceed to the next level in the relationship depends totally on the individual persons concerned and their respective mind-sets.

We however took great care of our friendship, treating it at par with *Gangajal*. We did absolutely nothing that could prove to be a blot on the pure relationship. Neither did we neither indulge in any socially unacceptable behaviour nor make an exhibition of it to draw unnecessary attention. At no time did we go public with our sentiments for each other. At times we may have ventured somewhere in quiet surroundings but were always discrete in our behaviour and took great care to maintain ourselves within the framework of social norms.

Once while relaxing on the sands of the river coast Siddharth took my hand in his and said 'We have met too late in life. Had we met at the right time I would have shown you how a man makes true love.'

I quickly released my hand from his warm clasp and taking the words in a casual manner, said, 'what rubbish are you talking?' Thank god it was dark; else he would surely have noticed the colour of blush on my face!

Siddharth would surely have proved himself – a true lover! He was so good and understanding by nature. Had destiny brought us together at the right time I would surely have been so fortunate in love! But there was no use regretting it now. I had come a long way in life since then, and now at this juncture I was determined to treasure the happy moments. Siddharth's company was all I needed to fulfil

---

Gangajal – According to Hindus, Water from Ganges is very Auspicious and Holy.

my craving for happiness. Instead of getting entangled in the thoughts about my past life I would rather choose happiness in the present moments. Instead of nurturing joyous dreams for the future I had an urgency to grab whatever happiness was there before me at this moment.

'Why! If you didn't like what I said, I'm sorry', he said sympathetically.

It was my turn to soothe him. 'Not at all, Siddharth! But what's the point in this wishful thinking?'

Then Siddharth said, 'Okay, okay, ma'am, you are right!', and then laughingly changed the topic.

After the summer vacations it was the first day of college. The last two months had experienced a very hot summer. But it was restful too. The only stress was that of the papers sent by the university to check for valuation. Over the last two months I had become so accustomed to this leisurely way of life. However, from today onwards it was back to the practice of getting up early, rushing to catch the train, the usual hustle and bustle in the morning with life once again reverting to the set routine. The pleasant and the not-so-pleasant faces would once again be visible after a gap of two months. The pleasant faces were those of some of my friends as well as students. And one special face amongst them was that of Siddharth. For me Siddharth was a genius. He was one person in the world for a glimpse of whom I would get sick with yearning. I had realised love through the companionship of Siddharth. I had now left behind my loathing for the entire male species of the world only because of Siddharth's behaviour.

I had started loving him without his being aware of it. In fact I too was unaware of it. According to Elaine Hatfield, the well-known psychologist, there are two basic types of love: One is compassionate love and another is passionate love. Compassionate love usually develops out of feelings of mutual respect for each other, attachment, affection and trust.

Passionate love is developed out of sexual attraction and intense affection emotions. People feel more happiness when cards of intense affection played from both the sides. These passionate love relations are generally for a short period and are temporary one.

During the vacations too I was obsessed with Siddharth and in the last week I yearned to meet him. I could not wait to see him, to be with him. I felt this time when we met I would admit my feelings to him and be done with it. Stifling one's feelings – was this not a form of violence?

The first day was comparatively free and was mostly spent in chitchatting with colleagues. But there was a regret at the end of the journey and that was on account of Siddharth. Siddharth was nowhere, either at the station or in the train.

I continued to feel low even after I reached home and threw myself on the bed. I was not in a mood to do anything. With no exhaustion whatsoever, there was no question of falling asleep. I just lay on the bed doing nothing. The fan was whirling above me, spreading its breeze all over the place. It was impossible to stay indoors without a fan. But at times the sound of the breeze disturbed me. It became a source of annoyance. When the mind is feeling run down and sad then even the things that generally fall under the definition of happiness, appear to be disturbing. When in sorrow one does not care a fig about whether the sweat is dripping from the face or if the clothes one is wearing are fresh or not. We just feel like turning all the lights off and lying down just the way we are! Even though hungry, there is no urge to eat, no taste for food. That's how I was feeling today. Love is such a painful emotion. Even the memory of Siddharth was painful. Just like the fan whirling above, the memories started churning inside my head; not slowly, but with tremendous speed!

Siddharth was not there today but he would certainly be there tomorrow, I tried to pacify myself. But my mind was in no mood to listen. A profound loneliness swept over me. At such a time I was left with no other option but to go over the memories of the many occasions that I had spent in his company. I remembered so many casual incidents and the joy that each of them brought me was enough to soothe my present misery, bringing a smile over my sad face.

There was one incident that I particularly remembered. Once I had gone on a long drive with Siddharth when he suggested that we go and explore a manganese mine. Of course I readily agreed. Since he knew the people at the mine we got the permission to see it. The mine was under caste and the manganese ore was extracted by excavating deep under the ground. Generally outsiders are not permitted to go in and see their underground operations. Moreover, entering mines is a risky affair and therefore permissions are hard to come by, especially for women. But Siddharth liked visiting such unusual places and was keen to take me along. He therefore made special efforts to obtain the permission for the both of us. We went eight hundred feet underground by lift in a weird form. We had to wear helmets with a light on it. Carrying a light was a necessity when going down in the midst of all the digging work. Walking with a lit up helmet one felt like a railway engine walking on its two feet. Even today when I think of that day eight hundred feet under the ground, I get goose pimples. I was so scared at that time but it was reassuring being in the company of Siddharth.

In that narrow path inside the mine it was darkness on all sides. With the light of my helmet I could only focus on Siddharth walking in front of me. One of the employees of the mine was walking in front of him. He was explaining the operations to us like a guide and accompanying us ahead. For the mining workers going in and out of mines was a routine affair and they appeared quite comfortable about it. However I was terrified. But with Siddharth around I mustered the courage to face the ordeal.

Another adventurous occasion that comes to my mind was when we had gone to the *Wainganga* River. The sun was setting and its red glow was spread across the skies. *Wainganga* had a deep and huge riverbed. The fisher folk had finished their daily chores and after tying up their boats on the coast were preparing to leave for home. Siddharth requested a fisherman to take the two of us for a round through the huge river expanse. The fisherman had already fastened his boat and was preparing to leave; but on Siddharth's persuasion he finally agreed to take us. The boat appeared too tiny to take us around the huge riverbed. The entire boat shook the moment I stepped on it. And when Siddharth came in it shook so hard that it almost flipped on the coast itself! Even before we made a start I was petrified. The fisherman told us not to get scared; it always shook that way. Both of us sat on a plank at one end of the boat and the fisherman sat at the other end and rowed the boat. Gradually the boat was advancing towards the middle of the huge riverbed. The coast retreated further away and the sky had acquired a darker shade. The evening was gradually turning into night. When we were at the coast we could see a few people around but now the coast was left far behind. The fishermen must have left for home and the coast was looking deserted. In the twilight only the sand was visible on the coast. We sat silently in the boat staring at the skies and at either sides of the river in turns. Observing nature set the thoughts flowing in the mind. The sound of waters splashing by the rowing paddles set the back ground score for my thoughts. That was the only audible sound in those surroundings. The seaman too rowed the boat in silence. The red glow in the sky had started dispersing lending a dark eerie shade to the waters. After a long while I broke the silence.

Siddharth, we have come a long way from the shore. How deep do you think this water is?'

Before Siddharth could answer the seaman said, '*Tai* (sister), this is the deepest side. The water should be around hundred to one fifty feet deep and that's why it is so still… like a lake.'

I was terrified on hearing this. My heart almost stopped beating. I looked at Siddharth and said, 'Let's go back now. It's getting very dark and I'm really scared.'

Siddharth held my hand and said courageously, 'Yes, you are really looking scared. But don't get scared. Nothing will happen.'

And with that he signalled he seaman to turn back.

It was not possible to gauge the depth of the water in the riverbed. Due to its excessive depth the flow of the water was not noticeable. Although the river was flowing it appeared still on the surface. Siddharth was with me and was quite courageous, but I was not sure of my destiny. I never knew when it would suddenly let me down. Siddharth, the seaman and I, only the three of us were there right in the centre of the huge riverbed at the surface of the 150 ft deep water. In case of any eventuality there was no one who could come to our rescue. Even though Siddharth knew swimming there was no guarantee that he would be in a position to swim to safety taking me along through the deep waters. For the seaman it was a routine affair and there was no question of any danger to him. As compared to the huge *Wainganga* River the boat appeared so tiny that it looked like a small wooden floating article. It was so rickety that even a heavy breath would have shaken it. Even breathing had to be gentle and controlled. This was my first adventure ride in a boat. Before we entered the river and for a while thereafter it was all quite enjoyable. But as evening started changing the ambience, words like thrill, adventure, beauty of nature, etc. were completely out of my mind. Living amidst the hustle and bustle of city life we are no wonder always on a look out for peace and quiet in natural surroundings. However the present dead stillness of the huge river was of a dreary, eerie kind. I carried the worst fears in my mind and yearned to return to the shore. Siddharth was with me and his presence was reassuring no doubt. But while floating at the mercy of a small wooden article on the surface of one fifty feet deep water, the fear gnawing at my heart just would not let go of me. At long last the boat finally touched the shore and I gave a deep sigh of relief. I was pitching dark all around. Even the sand under the feet was not visible; it was so dark. After paying the seaman we started towards the car.

Immediately on entering the car Siddharth put on the dim light inside the car. And when we saw the expressions on each other's faces, we burst out laughing.

'Kama,on whose assurance did you venture out into such deep waters?' Siddharth joked.

'Yours, Siddharth, yours!' I replied naughtily.

Siddharth continued, 'honestly, when I heard of the one fifty feet water, I myself had lost courage!' and once again we had burst out laughing. The memory is still fresh in my mind.

Even now I feel as if both the hazardous incidents had taken place may be just a couple of days back. Siddharth's bold and intellectual trait, his enthusiasm for trying out new things, his humorous, naughty nature under the façade of seriousness, charmed me no end.

My daily routine continued as usual. I would go to the station every day and continued with the train journey. A couple of months had elapsed and still there was no news of Siddharth. Earlier I used to be a depressed person by nature but my friendship with Siddharth had brought about a change in me. And now once again I was back to my old gloomy self. Walking across the station platform, the train journey, my work – I just had no interest in anything. My loneliness in the train and at home was spent mulling over the various occasions spent in the company of Siddharth. At the time when due to official problems our salaries were held back for two to three months, Siddharth had come to our place at ten in the night to help out with money matters. Once in the heat of summer the water pipe in our residential complex had burst and there was no water for drinking, cooking or bathing. When Siddharth came to know of this he himself had come over carrying Bislery cans and fresh food from hotel to our house. These were small incidents that I have treasured in my memory. There were many such incidents that brought to the fore the charitable nature in

Siddharth's otherwise solemn exterior and his eagerness to help out in times of need. I would remember such occasions, his company in the course of such incidents, my interactions with him during those times and thus the incidents would once again get refreshed in my memory. Engrossed in his memories I would find temporary relief from my sorrows, pains to a great extent.

After a couple of months, all of a sudden one day I saw a small letter from Siddharth in my letter box. Siddharth had written that he had been promoted and sent on deputation to the north east province by the central government for five years. As he had been given a promotion, he could not refuse the posting. The relocation had disturbed his family, children's education, etc. …etc.

The episode of my one sided affair had thus come to an end. Sometimes a stray thought would occur to my mind. Would it have been better had I admitted my love to Siddharth? Would he have responded positively? Whether it would have been ethical or not! It was so late now, but still Siddharth had taken the trouble to write and let me know. And in any case the affair had to end now. I was helpless. There was nothing that I held against Siddharth. I had loved him from my heart. May he achieve success all his life! I prayed silently as I lay in the bed. Drowned in his memories I did not realise when it was past 11. The eyelids weighed down as I continued to mutter, 'I love you, Siddharth, I love you! I love you!'

FATHER

Once mother had come over from the village to stay with me. She was with me for a good fifteen to twenty days. She would often come to stay with me. I being the only daughter she was quite attached to me. She was very fond of my son as well and loved buying expensive dresses and pampers him. Whenever she was here we would often go out for dinner together; just for a change, for her and for me as well.

My mother had been through a very hard life. When my father retired from government services he went off to the village all by himself. He had wanted mother to come with him, but his drinking habit had persisted even after his retirement and my mother clearly refused to accompany him. Actually it is during the post-retirement period that husband and wife need and are dependent on each other the most. This is the time they need love and care from each other, to relive the memories of the life spent in togetherness, to appreciate each other's achievements after having gone through the vagaries of life. By then they have already experienced joys and sorrows, and been through so many misfortunes together. Happiness followed by sorrow, and then happiness again…. Human life is based on this cycle of nature. Period of sorrow is akin to a dark night. And after the dark night there is always a happy and bright morning waiting for us. This is a law of nature. That's how after every experience of sorrow the ensuing happiness invigorates the mind. This is an important lesson of life. These ups and downs are the basis on which human life unfolds. The way an expensive brocade border enhances the beauty of a saree, similarly life too needs a beautiful border. Unfortunately my parents were not destined for it.

One day we got the news that father had collapsed on the farm. My brother, I and other relatives rushed to the village. The neighbours had already admitted him to a hospital. As soon as we reached there my brother arranged to transfer him to a better district hospital. On seeing the state of my father tears welled up in my eyes. He had been reduced to a skeleton. Liquor had taken its toll and not left an iota of flesh on his body. It was a dead body alive for a few more days. The doctor had put him on saline at the hospital and started treatment. *Tatya* (father) was in sedation for the entire night. In the morning he tried raising his heavy eyelids. He looked at the three of us, my mother, my brother and me, as we were standing beside his bed. The remorse of having compromised on his duty as a father and the acute sorrow of not bringing any happiness to his wish could not remain hidden in those pathetic eyes. Tears started flowing from his eyes and my mother and I too could not control our sobs. I was pressing *Tatya*'s feet and said, '*Tatya*, please relax'. Mother was moving her hand over his head and my brother was watching the three of us in turns. He was perhaps at a loss of words to say anything or comfort anyone.

Tatya – Elder persons are respectfully called as Tatya.

Tatya had given up food since the last four days, said the neighbours. Perhaps he was holding on to life so that he could meet us for the last time. The doctor had told my brother that there no hope and he could pass away anytime now. No matter what kind of life *Tatya* had led, at the end of the day he was my father. And that my father was leaving me for good and going away made me feel extremely sad. It was true that till now I had not maintained any relation with him; but still the awareness that I had a father somewhere in the world, was always at the back of my mind. Now *Tatya's* time was up. Someone so close going away from us was a scary thought; it was difficult to swallow. Mother's condition was no different from mine. No matter where *Tatya* was, she had always applied vermillion on her forehead in his name.

I called up Guruji and informed him about *Tatya's* health. Guruji too was saddened on hearing about the condition of *Tatya* in his final hours. He said he was leaving immediately for here. But the travelling itself would take two to two and half hours.

Guruji continued over the phone, 'Kama, do you remember we spoke about what goes on in the mind of a person when he is on his deathbed?'

I said, 'Yes, Guruji'.

Vermillion Applied on forehead – Vermillion is used as Sindoor. Sindoor is traditionally applied as a dot on the forehead by woman. Sindoor is the mark of a married woman in Hinduism. Widows do not wear sindoor, signifying that their husband is no longer alive.

Guruji said, 'Now that *Tatya* is all set to leave on his final journey see that you behave in such a way that he feels happy, joyful and contented. I'll be right there'.

I remembered Guruji's words. At the time of birth the soul is absolutely pure, clean and peaceful. But in the course of the various trials and tribulations of life it is exposed to good and bad influences. Laying on his death bed a person goes through the entire episode of his life and reviews the role he has played in it, along with his good and bad deeds. His misdeeds are a source of profound remorse to him, and moreover, there is hardly any time left to make amends. There is nothing he can do to rectify things no matter how much he yearns to do so because his senses are no longer in a position to support him. He feels extremely dejected due to this. At such a time the person longs to ask for forgiveness for his mistakes. At the same time he is also willing to forgive others for their mistakes. During this final stage the soul tries to free itself from its emotional ties and return to its original form. We come to this world empty handed and return empty handed. Thus at the end he does not want to carry any baggage of his mistakes or pardons along with him. He wishes to be forgiven for his mistakes by his near and dear ones just as he himself has forgiven everybody else. That is why Guruji had said that one should not harbour any ill will or enmity towards a departing person. The person on his death bed may appear silent but his soul is alert and watchful. As the body gets increasingly weaker the soul is compelled to leave it. Towards the end until the time the soul leaves the body there is a sudden awakening of the consciousness experienced by the person on his death bed which enables him to acutely feel the presence of the people around him and also sense the good or bad feelings towards him nurtured in their minds. That is why you will find some people reciting *Sunderkand* from Ramayana. The object is to purify the soul on its onward journey to the next world.

In the morning *Tatya* had opened his eyes to have a look at us. Perhaps he wished to see us again and again and that is why he was trying to open his heavy eyelids. However he could not open his eyes fully. Apparently he wanted to speak to us at length but his lips kept quivering and were unable to form the words. In between we were calling out to him loudly in a pathetic effort to wake him up; but his only response was 'Hmm'.

After his two hour journey Guruji finally arrived at the hospital. He drew his hand over *Tatya*'s eyes and called out loudly '*Tatya, Tatya!*'

Tatya once again uttered 'Hmm' and tried opening his eyes, but they would not open. Guruji had brought *Gangajal* with him.

In India it is customary to offer *Gangajal* (Water from Ganga River) to a person in his last moments on the deathbed. No other water on earth is as pure as *Gangajal*. It is believed that drinking water from the Ganges at the time of death would cleanse the impure soul.

It is auspicious to drink the Gangajal in the hour before death. As we have seen, this river holds a special significance in the hearts of Hindus. The ancient scriptures mention

---

Sunderkand from Ramayana – Hanuman was fondly called Sundar by his mother AnjaniMata and Sage Valmiki preferred this name for this fifth chapter of Ramayana. Sunder kand deals mainly with Hanuman's journey to Lanka in the search of Sita the wife of Lord Rama.The original *Sundara* Kanda is in Sanskrit and was composed by Valmiki, who was the first to scripturally record the *Ramayana*.

that the water of Ganges carries the blessings of Lord Vishnu's feet. On the journey back home from the Ganges, we Indians carry small quantities of river water with them for use in rituals. When a loved one dies, Hindus bring the ashes of the deceased person to the Ganges River. The Ganges is the embodiment of all sacred waters in Hindu mythology. The rivers of India are the main source of living of the Indian people because of their spiritual significance. Water from the Ganga has the unusual property that any water mixed with even the smallest quantity of Ganga water becomes Ganga water, and inherits its healing and other holy properties! Some Hindus also believe life is incomplete without bathing in the Ganga at least once in one's lifetime. Many Hindu families keep a vial of water from the Ganga in their house. This is done because it is prestigious to have water of the Holy Ganga in the house, and also so that if someone is dying, that person will be able to drink its water. Many Hindus believe that the water from the Ganga can cleanse a person's soul of all past sins...

For Hindus in India, the Ganga is not just a river but a mother, a goddess, a tradition, a culture and much more.

Guruji guided my mother, brother and me to feed *Tatya* spoonful each of the *Gangajal* and we did so.

I said in my mind, '*Tatya*, we could not bring you any form of happiness during your lifetime. Please forgive me.' *Bhau* and mother fed him *gangajal* with teary eyes. They too must have had similar sentiments.

It was evening now and the twittering of the birds had increased considerably. The hospital premises were surrounded by huge old trees. When our near and dear ones gather in a place there is so much thronging and they create such a racket. The same way the birds which had left their nests and flown away for the entire day were now back with their kith and kin. They had crowded the trees and there was plenty of chirping, as if they had come to meet *Tatya*. But here was soul of *Tatya*, preparing to leave its own nest!

The evening was getting increasingly darker. Looking out from the hospital window it appeared totally dark. For some unknown reason the nightfall appeared very scary. The birds had by now retired to their nests and the ambience turned amazingly quiet. My mother, brother, Guruji and I were sitting silently around *Tatya's* bed. There was no talking amongst us; we were just sitting and staring blankly at nothing. All of a sudden there was a loud sound of sob from *Tatya*. At once all of us sprang to our feet. My brother quickly took hold of *Tatya's* wrist; maybe he was checking the pulse. He already knew what there was to know. He turned the regulating latch of the saline. I was apprehensive. Rushing outside he called out to the nurse and the doctor on duty. Both of them told us to stay away for a while. We could see brother checking *Tatya* along with the doctor.

In a couple of minutes after checking the doctor and the nurse removed the saline and put the stand aside. My brother's eyes were filled with tears. We already knew what had happened. *Tatya* was no more. Mother and I were weeping. Mother started wailing and dropped her head on *Tatya's* legs. I held *Bhau* close and wept. *Bhau* was crying too but kept drawing his hand over my back to console me. Guruji was sitting silently on a stool with his head thrown down.

RAGHU

That was a Saturday, the 2nd of May! As usual on that day too I had gone to the Hanumanji temple to pay my obeisance. However, unlike at other times, it was in a severely depressed state of mind that I returned home after paying obeisance to Hanumanta. It was my usual practice to carry flowers, garlands, etc. for the deity whenever I visited the temple. There is a certain shop where I have been purchasing these things over the last so many years. However the shop at the entrance of the temple was closed on that particular day and I had no choice but to buy all the flowers, garlands, etc. from the adjacent shop. I casually enquired with the shopkeeper as to why the next door shop was closed.

He replied, 'Raghu passed away today!'

I exclaimed, 'passed away? What do you mean?'

He replied, 'Oh sister, he's expired!' I mumbled, 'meaning….?' I was stunned into silence. I just could not believe him; it was unbelievable!

The shopkeeper broke the silence. 'Sister, when we got the news in the morning we too couldn't believe it! But Raghu is not with us anymore. Yes…. it is true!' He wiped the corners of his eyes.

I said, 'It was only on last Saturday that he had given me flowers and garlands.'

The shopkeeper replied, 'Yes sister, all of us know you have been religiously coming to the temple for the last so many years and purchasing flowers and garlands only from Raghu.'

In fact I have been visiting this Hanumanji temple every Saturday religiously, without fail. Many years ago I had left our village and migrated to this city for work. Just as every village had its own particular goddess that looked after its people and protected them, somewhat on the same lines it was my simple belief that in my place of work in this urban area, this was my God. This ancient and bustling temple of Hanumanji was the epicentre of spiritual support to the residents of the city. I experienced profound sense of peace and contentment whenever I visited this place. I had decided that so long as I was in the city I would visit and pay my obeisance at this temple every Saturday.

In our lives we make so many resolutions but do not necessarily live up to them. Even great efforts and determination sometimes fail to fulfil our aspirations. I believe that all our efforts and determination should have the blessings of providence; else all our aspirations are merely a waste of time! I had made up my mind to visit the Hanumanji temple on Saturdays. May be that had divine support! By Hanumanta's grace I could offer my prayers at the temple every Saturday. I am fortunate that Hanumanta had granted me shelter at his feet; I am a blessed soul! It is indeed a divine privilege that I am considered worthy enough to worship him. There are many who are willing to serve God, but for Him to accept one's devotion and service was indeed very fortuitous. For my God, I was the chosen one for this honour!

Over the past so many years I have been visiting the Hanuman temple religiously on Saturdays. Paying obeisance to the divine Hanumanta has been inculcated as a matter of routine discipline in my life. Come Saturday and without fail my feet would head towards the Hanumanta temple. For some reason if I am late for the temple, I become extremely restless. The gates of the temple close at 10:30 in the night after prayers. I have made it to the temple even as late as 10:30. I return from the temple in a peaceful frame of mind. I am filled with happiness and engulfed in divine spiritual bliss!

My relationship with this supreme God is akin to that of a close relative. He is like a close family member. Perhaps that might be so because of my constant preoccupation with him. There is great significance attached to Hanumanta. It is impossible to define our relationship in words as in the case of other familial relations. On account of the limitations in verbal expression I do not wish to lessen the importance or the divinity of this God in any manner. The affinity is somewhat similar to what you experience towards a personality that evokes deep love and admiration in you. This is the kind of bond that I share with my God. Earlier I would address him as Hanumanji but now it is an informal Hanumanta! We have now established a rapport!

The first time I went to the Hanuman temple on a Saturday. I stood in front of the flower shop at the temple gate. The shop belonged to Raghu. Right from day one I purchased flowers and garlands from Raghu and this eventually became a matter of routine practice. Whenever coming to pay my obeisance I would come and stand in front of Raghu's shop, reciting *Hanuman chalisa* in my mind. There would be no interruption in my silent incantation as I stood there and of his own accord Raghu would hand over the flowers and garlands to me. I would then stand in front of Hanumanta, place my offerings in front of him and presumed that my prayers would be accepted. Whenever I stood in front of Raghu's shop I got a feeling of being treated like a VIP; because in spite of there being other customers he would cater to me preferentially, taking care not to disturb me in my prayers. I thought Hanumanta himself had placed Raghu at the gate to welcome and serve me. Raghu would be so prompt in attending to me as though he had been trained by Hanumant himself to do so. Probably Raghu too was an ardent devotee of Hanumanta. He did not miss a single opportunity to welcome me. This went on not only for a couple of years but for the past many years. At times when Raghu was not in, his wife or son would attend to me. Whenever he missed me thus, he would remember the incidence the next time we met, 'Sister, didn't see you last week!'

Many a times I got a feeling that Hanumanta himself was present in the form of Raghu and speaking through him. When he wasn't there, I felt my visit to Hanumanta was incomplete. I think Raghu was the greatest devotee of Hanumanta. Right from 5 or 7 in the morning up to 10 in the night he would supply puja material to the devotees at modest costs. Service to the devotees was tantamount to service to God.

From now onwards Raghu would never be seen or met again. The thought was enough to bring tears to my eyes. Taking hold of myself I started the car and headed towards home with a sad and heavy heart. My mind remained focussed on Raghu as I chanted *Hanuman chalisa* in silence.

Satsang and Introspection

'Guruji, it's been quite a while since I attended *satsang* last. And yes, we're always using this word *'satsang'*; what is exactly meant by satsang?' I asked.

Guruji replied, 'That's true. We are always doing *satsang*. Let's discuss the subject of *satsang* today. 'Sat' means truth and 'sang' means 'in the company of'. In other words, when we are in the company of truth, we are into *satsang*. In this world where do we find truth? It is definitely with those who have experienced truth or those who have totally surrendered themselves to the service of God or those endowed with spiritual wisdom. When spiritual interaction with such people evokes an experience of pure ideological vibrations, it is known as *satsang*.

Such vibrations can also be experienced In the course of *bhajans, kirtans* or in temples. So *bhajans, kirtans*, visiting temples or group meditations all come under the purview of *satsang*. *Satsang* enables us to derive happiness by getting involved in the flow of spiritual thoughts. It also facilitates

---

Bhajan – Religious poems and songs
Kirtan – Religious discourse

in making our thought process increasingly positive, strong, pure and inspiring.

As mentioned earlier *satsang* means being associated with the truth. Going deeper into the subject on the basis of spirituality, I may even add that *satsang* also encompasses a state of consciousness that is associated with qualities of truth, purity, etc; because one who imbibes these qualities is endowed with wisdom and is perpetually engaged in a spiritual dialogue with his own self. Whether by himself or in company, he is always in the state of *satsang,* experiencing divine power. When you are in meditation you are able to become detached from yourself and observe yourself and your actions. With meditation it becomes possible to peep into your own consciousness. They say befriending oneself is equivalent to befriending God. In my opinion this experiences constitutes the highest form of *satsang.*

When in the company of enlightened souls we are able to sense the vibrations emanating from them in the atmosphere. These vibrations start having an influence on our minds without our being aware of it. Often we go through this experience when sitting in solitude in a holy place. When in contact with such mystical vibrations we experience a feeling of renewed exuberance. One experiences the bliss of extraordinary peace and wisdom, as well as cleansing of the mind. Divine thoughts start flowing into the consciousness. The consciousness is illuminated and we are spurred on the path in search of truth. This may be termed as a spiritual friendship or a special association. And this *satsang* eventually paves the way for establishing friendship with God.

Friendship with God is a unique and the highest form of *satsang.* Experiencing God through the medium of thoughts, words and deeds, chanting incantations, sacrifices, love, kindness and knowledge obtained from a teacher are the various ways to connect with God. The feeling of total surrender to God is in itself the supreme form of *satsang* with God.

'*Nase Rog Hare Sab Pira Japat Nirantar Hanumat Bira.*'—These beautiful lines are from *Hanuman Chalisa* written by Sant Tulsidas. They are so full of faith and reassurance. Worshiping Hanuman and chanting his name constantly destroys diseases and removes all miseries. Thank God! Guruji had introduced the *Hanuman Chalisa* in my daily routine, in my conduct. Until such time as we do not get the royal status or a high status, we do not understand the importance of the line '*Ram Milay Rajpad Dinha.*' So long as we do not face difficulties we do not understand the meaning of the lines '*Sankat Te Hanuman Chhudawe Man Kram Bachan Dhyan Jo Lawe.*' The 40 verses of the *Hanuman Chalisa* are simply brilliant. They are 40 chants. Even when we are experiencing happiness or joy we wonder if it would be snatched away from us. At such times the following *Hanuman Chalisa* lines immediately come to the lips. '*Sab Sukh Lahe Tumhari Sarna Tum Rakshak Kahu Ko Darna.*' You are the cause of all happiness and since you are the protector no one dare to take it away from me. Why should I worry? Saying '*Buddhhi Hin Tanu Janike Sumiro Pawan Kumar.*' in the beginning you (the God) destroy the ego completely. "God *Hanumanji,* I am ignorant,' said in good faith, will make it impossible for the ego to thrive. When this is followed by '*Bal Buddhi Vidhya Dehu Mohi Harahu Kalesh Bikar.*' strength, wisdom and knowledge start entering our beings with the same speed at which the ego was destroyed. The strength, wisdom and knowledge from Hanuman are in egoless form and put an end to all miseries and afflictions.

Every line of the *Hanuman Chalisa* is exquisite. It is exuberant, radiant and amazing. It is magical in the sense that it has the power to make a change in life.

As regards '*Sankat Te Hanuman Chhudawe Man Kram Bachan Dhyan Jo Lawe*', an ordinary person with limited intelligence like me would have a restricted interpretation that if you with your life, words and deeds adapt the *Hanumant* principles in your behaviour then *Hanumanji* would free you from any adversity.

But world sage, Morari Bapu, in one of his lectures had clarified the logic behind this verse. *Bapu* says, 'the biggest calamity in our life can be avoided by simply worshiping *Hanumanji* and chanting his name'. He further says, 'In spite of having the time and the capacity, we are still not able to worship, chant or serve, then take it that we are in trouble.'

I pay my obeisance to the universal saint, *Hanumant* devotee, Morari Bapu.

'WHO IS A SADGURU?'

Mother had come from the village to stay with me. Shyam was appearing for the eighth standard exams and mother was going to stay with us till her exams were over. Once when Shyam was doing his maths homework he was stuck with a problem. He explained it to me and wanted my help in sorting it out. I tried but could not solve it. Mathematics was not my cup of tea. But Shyam was so adamant by nature! Once his mind was set on something he had to have it at once. As usual he insisted on the problem to be solved, and solved immediately. Mother suggested that I call Guruji in the evening and get the problem solved by him. That would also give her a chance to meet him.

Accordingly I called up Guruji and invited him over to our place in the evening. For the last many months I had been following the religious, spiritual path as advised by him. The change that had come over my day to day life, in my nature was obvious to my mother. There was a phenomenal change in my behaviour. I was fed up of struggling with my life made miserable by so many unfortunate events. Everyone had earlier noticed my pessimistic, worried, sad and dull countenance. But ever since I started on the religious, spiritual path as indicated by Guruji, I had been transformed into a happy, confident and optimistic person. Mother had noticed the pessimism in my face now being replaced by a new optimism. My outlook on life had suddenly turned positive. Such new emotions were emerging from inside and were reflected in the face. May be this was the divine glow. Guruji had introduced new exuberance in the darkness of my life. This Guruji had come into my life as a guide, as a messenger of God. My mother too was very keen to meet this divine person.

Guruji arrived at our place around 7:30 in the evening. Mother was sitting in the drawing room when he arrived. Immediately on entering Guruji touched mother's feet. He did not even wait for me to come and introduce them. He must have guessed the aged lady sitting in the drawing room to be my mother; or maybe he subscribed to a culture where elders were greeted in this manner. Whenever Guruji came to my house he would invariably occupy one of the two plastic chairs that were kept in a position facing east. There was a big sofa set in the drawing room as well, but Guruji stuck to the plastic chair. It was a fetish with him. Guruji would say, 'I sit here as in this position I face the east. And I don't know why but I feel very comfortable sitting on this plastic chair.'

Guruji always maintained a cheerful disposition. As he took his place smilingly in the chair, I said to mother, 'Mom, this is our Guruji.' Guruji and mother both folded their hands and greeted each other.

It is customary in India to do *namaste*. When meeting for the first time or at any other time it is our custom to fold hands and do *namaste*. Foreigners are generally seen

---

Touching feet – In India, It is customary to touch feet of seniors as a mark of respect and Greeting & seek blessings

shaking hands. Nowadays, in India too shaking hands is gaining acceptance. However as this does not conform to our inherent culture we do not experience as much joy and interest by shaking hands. Perhaps that is why many people at first do a *namaste* with both hands and follow it up with a hand shake. This is in no way meant to belittle the alien practice of shaking hands. Every country goes by its own way of doing things. In fact I have read that shaking hands adds warmth to the contact. One can gauge the feelings of a person through the personal touch of a hand shake.

No sooner mother had mentioned the reason for calling Guruji, she called for Shyam and told him to check with Guruji and get his maths problem sorted out. Shyam instantly got his maths books to Guruji and in a short while his problems were solved.

For those ten to fifteen minutes mother was carefully observing Guruji - the way he spoke, his body language, his in-depth knowledge in maths, etc. Mother had spent sixty three years of her life in acute adversity. Going through the various phases she had mastered the art of understanding people. After having experienced life in its varied forms, towards the end one attains the ability to discern human behaviour accurately. In those ten to fifteen minutes without speaking to Guruji directly, mother had been able to assess his nature instantly. She was feeling happy from inside out.

I was busy in the kitchen when she came inside and said to me, 'I know your Guruji by now. Though I haven't spoken to him, I can say on the basis of my experience that he is a thorough gentleman and an excellent human being.'

What could I comment on that? All I knew was that Guruji had introduced me to religiousness. He taught me spirituality. He was free of addictions, selfless and had a helping nature. Whenever I faced any difficult situation in life he would be there to sincerely guide me on how to deal with it, how to go about in the circumstances. We considered him as close as a family member. In fact, Guruji was indeed our family member.

Mother continued further, 'His face has such a divine glow and he has such a blissful expression like a sage. His eyes sparkle like an enlightened soul. It is God's grace that such a wise Sadguru should visit our home of his own accord. It is God's grace that we have been blessed with such a Sadguru. Kama, honestly, I am speaking from my heart. He is a genuine Sadguru'.

In Sanskrit 'Gu' means 'darkness' and 'ru' means 'the one who removes'. So 'Guru' means one who removes darkness. And Sadguru means the guru who removes three types of darkness from human life. The three types are material, mental and spiritual. Every guru is not necessarily a Sadguru. Sadguru is the one who guides us on the spiritual path to comprehend the laws of life.

There are three types of gurus – those with basic, moderate and excellent knowledge. The first type of guru confines his duty only to giving advice. He does not consider it necessary to observe the response or the progress of the student, nor is he bothered about it.

While the second type of guru gives advice, he also tries to understand the problems faced by the student and guides him in resolving them. But he does not keep a check on the student or follow up in a disciplined manner.

The third type of guru, besides giving advice and guiding the student in resolving problems, also keeps a close watch on him and ensures that all instructions are followed till such time as his problems are resolved and he attains full progress. And thereafter he continues to guide the student for the rest of his life.

Bearing the material, mental and spiritual aspects in mind, when a guru guides the student in this manner and empowers him to achieve the supreme spiritual goal, he is called Sadguru. Efforts of a Sadguru are focussed on clearing the doubts in the mind of the student and making him conscious of achieving the supreme spiritual goal. One should understand that finding a true Sadguru is God's wish or a blessing of God. In fact, finding a true Sadguru is as good as achieving God.

Mere observing Guruji had made such a deep impression on my mother. It is believed that the presence of a Sadguru washes away all your misdeeds of the past many lives and relieves you of all sins. This is what I sensed from my mother's words. Mother, at least for the time being, appeared to have put all her sorrows behind her and looked happy as if relieved of all her sins of the bygone lives. A person may be able to hide his sorrows but it is not humanely possible to hide his joy. Happiness emanating from one's consciousness comes gushing out into the open like the waves of the sea. They are so genuine that no force is powerful enough to control them. The sea itself cannot stop the waves from springing up. Our ancient literature has at times been found to substitute the word 'Sadguru' by the word '*Satchchidanand*'. *Satchchidanand* stands for *sat+chitta+anand*. *Satchchidanand* must be existent in a Sadguru and this excessive bliss must

---

Satchchidanand stands for sat+chitta+anand. – Sat – indicates the truth
Chitta – State of mind
Anand – Spiritual Happiness, delight

be overflowing and immersing in it all those who came in contact with him. That is how it must be.

Mother said, 'Come out in the drawing room. Let's talk to Guruji'.

I replied, 'Yes, mother, you carry on; I'll join you.'

Mother was chatting with Guruji and told him in brief all about her past life. Tears welled up in her eyes when she apprised him about how in her life she had endured acute miseries, the tremendous difficulties she had to face when in spite of hailing from a tribal family she not only got educated herself but also saw her children through higher education. Guruji, in keeping with his nature, gave her a patient hearing. Having finished my work in the kitchen I came out and sat with my mother.

Mother continued, 'Guruji, until now I have never disclosed my sorrows before anyone. I never felt inclined to do so. I strongly felt that whatever sorrow my fate had destined for me had to be borne by me alone. At times I would confide in Kama. I don't know why, but since I set my eyes on you, I felt very close to you. I considered you as a close relative. Perhaps God had sent an angle in your form to understand and alleviate my sorrows.'

When speaking to Guruji if he was praised and if he thought it to be more than necessary, then he would put on a weird expression. He did not like being praised and now mother had gone to the extent of calling him as an angle!

Mother's condition was comparable to that of a vessel that had been cleared of sewage making room for pure water to come in.

One has to have someone close enough to be able to vent one's sorrows. That is human nature. There are many people at home, actual blood relations. But we cannot pour out our sorrows to each one of them. It is a rare one about whom we feel that he would listen to us patiently with due regards and would empathise with us. Unless we are sure of this we would never confide even with our family members. This brings us to certain profound truths about human nature. In keeping with his nature every person has a different set of sorrows. Their intensities vary too. We cannot put an end to others' sorrow but we can certainly reduce them. All we need to do is to lend them a patient and sympathetic hearing. A loving nature and compassion are the most crucial prerequisites for this. Love and compassion are such powerful emotions that they keep you stable and firm. This stability and firmness enables us to listen to others' sorrows with patience. The love and compassion flowing within us help us to alleviate others' sorrows and miraculously paves the way to create happy, blissful and vibrant sensations in them.

Isn't the stock of love and compassion inherent in us extraordinary and of paramount importance? Never allow this stock of love and compassion to exhaust. Everyone experiences happiness and sorrows in life. There are bound to be ups and downs. Life is an adventure and joys and sorrows are a part of that adventure. In times of happiness not letting the happiness go to one's head and during periods of sorrow facing the adversities squarely without getting disheartened, is by no means any less than any adventure. Since this is a natural flow of life, in both the circumstances one needs to master the art of remaining stable and maintaining equilibrium throughout one's life.

I would further add that this balanced way of living or learning to live one's life in this manner is confined to one's own life. Isn't it selfish to publicize one's sorrows, or seek solutions to one's own sorrows or problems, indulging in self-pity and capitalising on it to earn sympathy? We should remember that once we learn to handle our emotions and come out of them we are in a position to think about alleviating others' sorrows. For this it is necessary to develop a charitable disposition which enables us to empathise with others. Had I been in that person's place how would I have dealt with the situation? such are the thoughts that occur to the mind.

Two important things are vital for such charitable emotions to emerge in the mind and these are love and compassion. That is why, as stated earlier, never ever let the stock of love and compassion within you to exhaust. Consider it as your life-long savings. This is what enables us to live with humanity, alleviate other's sorrows and attain fulfilment our lives.

Love and compassion are inborn virtues in humans. Similar other virtuous qualities are also naturally existent within us. But the harsh realities encountered at every other step in life take their toll on these noble emotions. In fact going through the tough day to day situations we tend to forget our nobler qualities and hence these are not put to effective use. However, once we realise this treasure within us and use it appropriately then we can bring about tremendous happiness and fulfilment not only in our but others' lives too.

There was plenty to be learnt from such ideas mastered by Guruji. Guruji himself was an epitome of love and compassion. He would totally empathise when listening to the tragic happenings in others' lives. He would himself experience the sorrow and get overwhelmed by emotions. I have so often seen him choke with emotion. So often I have seen his eyes filled with tears. Some times Guruji would offer his guidance on how a particular tragedy could have been avoided or how to come out of it. And at times, when there was no way out, I have seen him feel helpless and saddened.

During my mother's sojourn with me she would often call Guruji over and discuss spiritual, religious and social issues with him. These discussions would go on for hours together. Mother would ask him clarifications on the various questions bothering her mind. Life is an unresolved riddle. There are many ups and downs one goes through in the course of life. At times we just about manage to handle them. Many a times we have struggled with the situations confronting us without sparing much thought, without applying our mind to it. We have seen the outcomes which are sometimes good too; but most of the times the results are unpleasant. During a critical situation an ordinary person is so fatigued confronting day to day situations that he has neither the time nor the inclination to think or study it at length. But after crossing the prime of our lives when such an occasion comes to our mind and we remember the way we dealt with the situation, we feel we should not have done what we did, behaved the way we did. The situation could have been handled in a different manner.

What wrong did I commit at that time? Was it possible to deal with the situation in any other manner? Or what I did then, was it the right thing to do? Was there no other option? etc… etc… Mother would try and remember the various incidents in her life and place them before Guruji. She would get Guruji to analyse the situations, the decisions taken at those times, the mistakes made, etc. and the conclusions arrived at would be as per her expectations.

Often when narrating the incidents mother would break down while at other times the humorous angle of the story made both, Guruji and mother, burst into peals of laughter. When evaluating the happenings in life each incident would end like an episode of a TV serial. Whatever happened was now over and gone. As regards her aspirations for the future, her responsibilities, mother would consistently seek Guruji's guidance, especially in order that the same mistakes were not repeated.

There used to be one persistent question from my mother: Is it possible to change our inherent nature? Can our nature be improved? When answering this, Guruji would invariably dwell on values and virtues that we subscribe to. It is these values and virtues that are responsible for our nature and attitude.

Values and virtues form our intrinsic treasure trove that enriches us. Values are like our pals and they are the ones that can bring us happiness. Subscribing to virtuous values gives rise to self-respect and dignity in our life. These values and virtues should be based on spirituality. We have to utilise these spiritual virtues in the material world. Virtues are the principles that enable us to evaluate the good and the bad aspects of our lives. Virtues are the restrictions that we place on ourselves for good behaviour and abiding by those rules. We may also add that patience, love, honesty, compassion and such other values are the benchmark of a virtuous person.

Good nature means building our character by taking care of our moral values. Developing one's sense of discretion on the basis of moral principles leads to character development.

Resoluteness and strong will power form the essential components of an enriched character. Loss of will power, loss of self-confidence, inability to take decisions, ethical dilemma is the main causes detrimental to good behaviour. In daily life our interactions with our relatives around us at home, or people we come in contact with outside in our workplace determine if our behaviour is good or bad. Our moral values are reflected through our behaviour in our interactions with people at home or outside. Getting rid of negative values, detrimental to our character and imbibing positive moral values herald the beginning of improvement in our nature.

Mother had narrated the various sorrowful, difficult, distressful situations in her life to Guruji. Through satsang with Guruji she had tried to find the causes of all her adversities. To a great extent the inferences drawn by Guruji in various matters were quite plausible. His experience of life and his in-depth knowledge of human nature were evident in his way of doing analysis and arriving at conclusions. Human nature is a mere play of emotions. When we hurt someone's feelings the ensuing turbulence in the emotions and the subsequent grave repercussions are an important issue which needs to be studied. It is the positive feelings in mind that create positive thoughts and therefore it is important that our actions should in no way cause ill feelings either in us or in others. On developing positive thinking one learns to sense happiness, sorrow, humiliation, feelings, etc in others and can correctly ascertain how to avoid the unpleasant incidents. Such a person while keeping himself aloof from situations of humiliations, sorrows, etc. is able to get down to the cause of such fleeting incidents and analyse them. Once it is possible to analyse them it becomes very easy to understand the nature of the other person. Most of the distressful situations in life can be traced to one's own wrong doings. Our good and bad actions are the product of our inherent nature. The impressions formed on our minds are the foundation on which our nature, our thoughts take shape.

Once I asked Guruji, 'I have always had a question in my mind'.

'What is it?' Guruji enquired.

I asked, 'how do you manage to find solutions to the different problems in everyone's life?'

My question implied a very serious and deep meaning. Guruji had convincingly resolved the issues bothering me in my life. In fact it was as if he had drawn up a scheme for me to follow in order that my future could be happy and joyful. I had developed the right attitude towards life only after the valuable *satsang* offered by Guruji from time to time. So many things had strangely turned out to be exactly conforming to Guruji's words. For instance, I felt I was not deserving enough and yet I had managed to get the highest degree like the PhD only because of the supernatural powers vested in Guruji. Moreover I had myself seen the experiences of my mother and my brother. In fact I have been a witness to them. We may call it as blind faith. But the fact is that faith is always blind; it does not see. And similarly trust also cannot see; that too is blind. In fact both the words fall in the blind category. Faith and trust are not possible with eyes open. One has to feel something in order to keep the faith, to trust. Else faith and trust are not possible in this world.

Mother had said to Guruji, 'I have endured plenty of sorrows in this world. Now that I am sixty four, I want to be very happy and rich too. I want to spend the rest of my life with dignity, prosperity and peace. And for that I already have my plans in place, but unfortunately, none of them turn out to be successful. They don't reach completion.'

To that Guruji had replied to mother, ' Now it's time you to retire from everything. Only then you will be able to allow happiness and peace in your life.'

Mother said, 'Guruji, I want to increase my savings and bring them to rupees eighteen lakhs in the next three years.'

Actually this question from my mother was aimed totally at worldly desires. In the spiritual context worldly desires are secondary while mental happiness and peace are given priority.

Nevertheless, Guruji replied, 'Yes, everything is possible. You will get what you want.'

And eventually things did turn out as per my mother's wish. At the end of three years my mother had called Guruji over and informed him about it. 'I don't know if I'm blessed by providence. But Guruji, today I have twenty lakhs with me! Now I am happy and peaceful in every way. Now I am in a position to help others in need. Now I have no more complaints in life.'

In the latter half of her life mother had got herself involved in social work. She had earned respect and status in society. She had adopted modern technology to cultivate the land inherited by her and was able to make a fortune. We had a huge plot of farming land but had no idea of its financial potential. The idea simply never occurred to any of us. Mother utilised this money to start an educational institution. Needy children from the tribal district thus got an opportunity to go for higher studies. Mother had thus made a name for herself in the entire region. But she would give the entire credit for this success to Guruji. 'It's Guruji's guidance that brought about this phenomenal change in my life,' she used to acknowledge so often.

My brother who was a doctor by profession, also held Guruji in high esteem. His medical clinic was his means of livelihood. He had decided to set up his dispensary in the tribal area in order to make good health care available to the people in the tribal district. Under the guise of health service, or rather simply service, most doctors ran their clinics with the singular agenda of doing business. When we exploit people under the pretext of doing service and parade ourselves as service givers, then somewhere it boils down to cheating the society. And we are so used to this rampant practice that we don't feel anything wrong about it. Moreover we have to create a place for ourselves amidst the medical fraternity and maintain the status. Every doctor cannot be expected to be a Dr Prakash Amte. That requires a temperament conductive to enormous sacrifice. No matter how educated a person is; it is important how cultured he is. In our pursuit of making money we tend to ignore the conscience within us. Once we let go of humanity, its adverse effects are felt first by the people around us and then it spreads across the society. We tend to ignore value based actions. Perhaps it may be possible to make money in that manner but we can never find happiness in life. All kinds of worldly pleasures, comforts can be bought with money but it cannot make us happy. It cannot get for us mental peace and happiness. Brother had made plenty of money but there was no happiness or peace at home. Conflict had become a permanent feature in his house. My sister-in-law was a doctor too but neither of them had the time to understand each other. Nor they think it as necessary. Money had taken the form of a poison.

But brother had seen a phenomenal change in the lives of my mother and me. People in this scientific age, who consider themselves as having a modern outlook, you will find them of tendency to poke fun at spirituality. They fight shy of adopting our age old, conventional, spiritual way of life. Even then, a couple of times my brother was present as a silent spectator when Guruji, mother and I were having our usual discussions.

There is a saying that even by mistake if we step on fire, the foot burns. And when the sun of wisdom arises, no matter how stark the darkness, it is bound to spread light. Brother did not find Guruji's spiritual thoughts as being out-dated. He appreciated Guruji's novel approach to life. Guruji explained significant things in a very casual manner. His style was simple and easy to follow. There was power in his words. His choice of words and ease of language took one on a trip through ecstasy. He listened patiently to everyone's sorrows, anxieties and then cheerfully and quietly made sincere efforts to offer his guidance and resolve the issues.

Whenever one apprised him of problems there was a feeling of belonging with him. My brother had made substantial amount of money and we were always under the impression that he must be leading a happy life. But he himself had poured out all his problems and sorrows to Guruji. Guruji gave him a patient hearing. I remember brother telling him at that time, 'Guruji, I'm feeling much better. Just by talking to you I feel as if all my problems are under control. I'm feeling so much lighter now.' Guruji had said, 'Doctor *Sahab*, everything will be fine. Don't worry.

You are in safe zone; God bless you.' Brother bent down to touch his feet but Guruji stopped him and shook his hands.

All the three of us, mother, brother and I, were getting consistent guidance from Guruji in our lives. Under Guruji's guidance brother's entire life style was transformed. His own nature also underwent a profound change. Conflicts in his personal life settled down. His life appeared to have undergone a phenomenal change.

'How do you find answers to everyone's difficult problems in life?' Guruji had no problem in answering the question put forward by me.

He began his explanation effortlessly. He said 'I am not endowed with any supernatural powers, nor do I subscribe to any kind of magic or witchcraft. When you all open up to me and narrate your problems, my initial reaction is that of acute sadness. I feel really miserable. Grief takes over me completely. And that is when my mind starts churning over the problem. I pray from my innermost self that you may overcome your sorrows and get empowered to face the situation. And you can see for yourself that as the sorrow wanes that's the beginning of happiness. Simultaneously I also appeal to you to do one thing, and that is, recite *Hanuman Chalisa*. Reciting *Hanuman Chalisa* on a regular basis creates tremendous positive energy. *Hanuman Chalisa* is an established divine incantation, the daily recitation of which increases self-confidence. It is a great help in getting rid of superstitions and purifying one's intellect, thoughts and actions. Once you acquire purity of soul and mind then it is followed by the end of ego. Destruction of the six vices gives us a new perspective to our problems and we become empowered to overcome the situation. Reciting the *Hanuman Chalisa* creates this tremendous magical power to bring about a change in one's character. You must have experienced the phenomenal changes taking place within you. I practice meditation every day. I remain in the meditational state in full concentration for a long time. Till such time as you get the expected results I continue with my meditation. The meditation invariably includes a prayer for the fulfilment of your aspirations. Wishes made with good will and selflessness come true one day. Any wish for others made with a pure heart proves itself to be the best wish. Through the medium of *Hanuman Chalisa* you tend to become a better human being. My concentration and pure intentions prove my wish to be the best for you which helps in bringing happy moments back in your life. This is my secret, Kama.'

Guruji had answered my question; however, I was not fully satisfied. No doubt what Guruji had said was true, but I was positive that there lay a divine treasure within Guruji. The constant influence of this divine power had made his spoken word so powerful. His simple and ordinary lifestyle made it impossible to comprehend the unlimited supernatural powers he was endowed with.

As Guruji had mentioned, it is true that wishes carry a lot of power. Good wishes!! Any kind of deliberation takes us to the core of the subject. It creates maturity within us. When we persistently wish someone well with pure and selfless intentions, it is equivalent to uttering incantations. By repeating incantations our sages and saints reaffirm the same and their penance empowers them to attain the desired results. Thus constant contemplation works like uttering incantations and reaches us to our desired goals. That calls for concentration. However, it is also important how strong, alert and aware our will power is.

At some point of time we all have come across practical examples of how powerful good wishes can turn out to be. For example, Amitabh Bachchan, the famous Indian actor, has crores of fans not only in India but all over the world. During the critical times of his near fatal accident crores of well-wishers round the world had simultaneously held prayers in temples, churches and masjids, eventually leading to his recovery from that accident. Famous cricketer, Yuvraj Singh, too recovered from an incurable disease like cancer as a result of the prayers offered by his many admirers. These fans are necessarily their genuine well-wishers. They have a great affection for their idols. Therefore sincere prayers, heartfelt good wishes coming from them are in no way any less than uttering incantations and as such are an accomplishment that enables strange and incredible results to materialise.

PURIFYING PROCESS

The six vices of passion, greed, hatred, lust, loathing and jealousy should be avoided in dealing with the outer world and similarly they should not be allowed to exist within our own consciousness either.

Being free of these emotions meant purification of our inner self. I had by now realised that unless I purified my mind with good and pure thoughts I will not be able to do meditation successfully so as to make any spiritual progress. So how do I get rid of negative thoughts and generate good and pure thoughts in my mind? I will have to create value based impressions on my mind. There should be a constant input of positive thoughts to the mind. I am reproducing Guruji's tips in this context.

At the outset we should learn to have faith in ourselves. One should stop thinking on the lines, ' nothing ever goes right with me', 'My future is doomed', and 'Even God can't save me from this ', ' No good will ever happen to me in this life', and so on. It is very important to have faith in oneself. Relax and move ahead. Bear in mind that every morning is a new morning for you, and wake up! Listen to your inner voice and abide by it. When stepping ahead towards a bright future do so with faith and confidence. For long term success qualities of perseverance, love, kindness and devotion are a must; so is hard work.

If you believe in your capabilities, if you are decided about taking the righteous path with sincerity and devotion, and if you have the ability to transform the passion within you into action, then you will know how to achieve success. In this endeavour even if there are hurdles in the way you will learn to get over them and succeed.

There should be a continuous awareness about what we are learning. Expecting success without any struggle is akin to going on a drive without expecting any potholes. No journey is easy. And here we are starting on an important journey for success in life.

Be realistic. Be determined to achieve success; yet at the same time do not entertain unrealistic expectations from life. We cannot force our will on life that we should always get exactly what we want. In your craving for a major happiness or success do not belittle minor achievements. In this important journey if you ignore the small joys and let them pass by, then the entire journey will turn out dull and unhappy. Even though the situations in this journey are not up to your expectations still learn to either enjoy them or accept them. There lies the fun of the journey. Take it as an adventure.

Instead of trying to drive out the negative thoughts, first try to bring in positive thoughts. Getting rid of vices from our consciousness will not happen overnight. Focus on how positive feelings can be inculcated. Whilst doing so you will not even realise the negativity being replaced by positive thoughts. Do not deplete your energy by carrying the baggage of waste thoughts like, what mistakes did I make in the past; why did they happen; had they not happened, I would have had a much better life, etc. Use the energy instead for creating positive thoughts that will facilitate your success in life.

Wait, watch and go – You are on an important journey leading towards success. It is said that distance lends a charm. Everything looks easy from a distance. On the contrary it is also true that certain things are easier to focus and appear clearer from a distance. Our success is camouflaged by our worries, doubts, disappointments, sufferings, etc. Don't we see the water level when we are neck deep in water? We have to learn to see likewise. In this journey you may encounter hardships but one is prepared to bear any pain for the sake of ultimate happiness, and don't think much of it. Similarly you should be able to easily forget the hardships. So stop, watch and then continue.

Success consists of going from failure to failure without loss of enthusiasm - Winston Churchill

Wait, turn around and look backwards. How much have you progressed in this journey? Is it really a progress? Analyse yourself. What are the challenges ahead? What are your goals? Keep reminding yourself time to time, again and again. Imagine how your mentor would have guided you had he been with you. You yourself are the observer and the witness in the present situation. Come out of yourself, be your own observer and think how you would guide yourself. Think of the similarities or the differences in your thinking pattern between your earlier thoughts and your guidance as an outside observer. There might not be much of a difference. Of the two the correct thoughts will be the ones backed by your intuition. Retreat and once again look at your aim. It will be clearer and more focussed from the new perspective. Now train your mind to resume the journey based on the intuition arising from the consciousness.

Value your emotions: The process of suppressing our emotions is a setback to our efforts. Sufferings borne by us in the past are an asset to us. The wounds inflicted on us by life are a hidden treasure which we can open and look at any time in solitude. It brings us immense happiness that we are the owners of such a huge, beautiful treasure. Today we got a chance to see the hidden treasure. Therefore do not suppress your emotions nor allow anyone else to do so.

You are not alone in this world. Even though you may be passing through a dark phase God invariably sends a guardian angel to be with you. You only have to look around to find who he is. Suppose its Guruji!! God must have sent him as his representative. Do not expect him to solve all your problems. Just open up and put before him what is worrying you. Trust him. Allow him to be with you. He may not be able to relieve you from the surrounding darkness but will surely be the twinkling lamp to help you find your way out. One thing you must bear in mind is that you are not alone. No matter how difficult the situation is, how gloomy the surroundings, God invariably sends someone to you, one who is as aware of your predicaments and difficulties as you are and who is willing to help you out. Now it is up to you to recognise him and put your trust in him. So now onwards you are not alone.

'Be optimistic. It is in darkness that you are able to spot the stars. This is a fact. Look at the stars; they signify hope. Also it is not advisable to be excessively optimistic and indulge in daydreaming. One may fill oneself to capacity with optimistic thoughts but efforts should also be made towards their sustenance and fulfilment. Although you may not have totally come out of your inherent pessimism, your new found hopes will enable you to take on the situations you are currently in. This will have a positive effect on your personality and make it easier to reach your desired destination.

Peace happens to be an integral part of our day to day life. But we are used to treating it like unattended trash lying in the corner and do not pay attention. Sit still for a while and focus your attention on that part of the brain. Look for peace and it will be there for you. Amidst the hustle and bustle of daily routine, some quiet and relaxation is a must. In life we have to get up and run around for so many things; but no efforts are required for peace, which can be experienced just by sitting in a place and relaxing. We should be equally passive and possessive about peace. We can start afresh only after relaxing completely, being completely quiet. Oh my past, I wish you goodbye. And thanks, for all the lessons that you have taught me! Stop thinking about the past and now…. over to the future! Because it is only after the first thing ends that the second can make a beginning. So try to see a beginning whenever there is an end. It is a natural phenomenon and supported by the laws of life that the point where something ends is also the beginning of something new.

Our behaviour meaning good conduct, honourable way of life, is imperative for purifying our consciousness. If we have clean character then it will reflect in our behaviour, and vice versa. Both are interdependent. To live an honourable life one has to inculcate certain basic moral values. What is exactly meant by values? As per the New Oxford Dictionary values are defined as 'a person's principles or standards of behaviour, one's judgement of what is important in life'. In other words values are the rules of behaviour one sets for oneself or the code of conduct decided by oneself for good behaviour.

Righteous behaviour is a must for making a success of life and attaining peace. For this we need to develop human values like cooperation, simplicity, honesty, unity, goodwill, morality, responsibility, etc. While doing this, without your even being aware of it, the consciousness will be free of all vices, making the mind clean and pure.

||HANUMAN CHALISA ||	**MEANING IN ENGLISH**

|| DOHA ||

Shri Guru Charan Saroj Raj	After cleansing the mirror of my mind with the holy
Nij manu mukuru sudhari	dust of divine Guru's Lotus feet. I describe the unblemished glory
Barnao Raghubar Bimal Jasu	of Shri Raghuvar which bestows the four-
Jo dayaku phal charee	fold fruits of life. (Dharma, Artha, Kama and Moksha).
Buddhi Hin Tanu Janike	Considering myself as intelligence less, I
Sumiro Pavan Kumar	concentrate my attention on Pavan Kumar (Lord Hanumanji)and
Bal budhi Vidya dehu mohee	humbly ask for strength, intelligence and true knowledge to
Harahu Kalesa Vikar	relieve me of all blemishes, causing pain.

||CHOUPAEE || (Verses)

Jai Hanuman gyan gun sagar	Victory to thee, O'Hanuman! Ocean of Wisdom-All
Jai Kapis tihun lok ujagar	hail to you O'Kapisa! (fountain-head of power,wisdom
	and Shiva-Shakti) You illuminate all the three worlds
	(Entire cosmos) with your glory.
Ram doot atulit bal dhama	You are the messenger of Shri Ram. The
Anjani-putra Pavan sut nama	repository of immeasurable strength, though known
	only as Son of Pavan (Wind), born of Anjani.
Mahavir Bikram Bajrangi	With Limbs as sturdy as Vajra (The mace of God Indra)

168

Kumati nivar sumati Ke sangi	you are valiant and brave. On you attends good Sense
	and Wisdom. You dispel the darkness of evil thoughts.
Kanchan baran biraj subesa	You are beautiful golden coloured and your dress
Kanan Kundal Kunchit Kesa	is pretty. You wear ear rings and have long curly hair.
Hath bajra Aur Dhwaja Viraje	You carry in your hand a lightening bolt along with a victory
Kandhe moonj janehu sajei	(kesari) flag and wear the sacred thread on your shoulder.
Sankar suvan kesari Nandan	As a descendant of Lord Shiva, you are a comfort and pride
Tej pratap maha jag vandan	of Shri Kesari. With the lustre of your Vast Sway, you are
	propitiated all over the universe.
Vidyawan guni ati chatur	You are learned in all the repository of learning, virtues and very clever,
Ram kaj karibe ko aatur	always eager to carry out the behest's of Shri Ram.
Prabu charitra sunibe ko rasiya	You enjoy listening to Lord Rama's story.
Ram Lakhan Sita man Basiya	Shri Ram, Lakshman and Sita always reside in your heart.
Sukshma roop dhari Sinyahi dikhava	You appeared before Sita in a Diminutive form and spoke to
Bikat roop dhari lanka jarava	her in humility. You assumed an awesome form and struck terror by setting Lanka on fire.
Bhima roop dhari asur sanhare	With over-whelming might you destroyed demons and performed

169

Ramachandra ke kaj sanvare	all tasks assigned to you by Shri Ram with great skill.
Laye Sanjivan Lakhan Jiyaye	You brought Sanjivani Mountain (A herb that revives life) to save
Shri Raghuvir Harashi ur laye	Lakshman's life. Shri Ram cheerfully embraced you with his heart full of joy.
Raghupati Kinhi bahut badai	Lord Shri Ram praised your excellence and
Tum mam priya Bharat-hi sam bhai	said: "You are as dear to me as my own brother Bharat."
Sahas badan tumharo yash gaave	Thousands of living beings are chanting hymns of your glories;
As kahi Shripati kantha lagaave	saying thus, Shri Ram warmly hugged him (Shri Hanuman).
Sankadik Brahmadi Muneesa	When royal sages like Sanaka, Lord Brahma, Narad himself, Goddess Saraswati and Adhishesa(one of immeasurable dimensions).
Narad Sarad sahit Aheesa	
Jam Kuber Digpal Jahan te	Even Yamraj (God of Death) Kuber (God of Wealth) and the
Kavi kovid kahi sake kahan te	Digpals (deputies guarding the four corners of the Universe)
	Can not describe your greatness properly. How then, can a mere poet
	give adequate expression of your super excellence.
Tum upkar Sugreevahin keenha	You helped Sugriva. You united him with
Ram milaye rajpad deenha	Shri Ram and he installed him on the Royal Throne.

Tumharo mantra Vibheeshan mana	Vibhishana accepted your suggestions and became Lord of Lanka.
Lankeshwar Bhaye Sub jag jana	This is known all over the Universe.
Yug sahastra yojan par Bhanu	On your own you dashed upon the Sun, which is at a fabulous
Leelyo tahi madhur phal janu	distance of thousands of miles, thinking it to be a sweet fruit.
Prabhu mudrika meli mukh mahee	Carrying the Lord's Signet Ring in your mouth, there is
Jaladhi langhi gaye achraj nahee	no wonder that you easily leapt across the ocean.
Durgaam kaj jagat ke jete	All difficult tasks of the world become easy
Sugam anugraha tumhre tete	with your kind grace.
Ram dware tum rakhvare,	You are the sentry at the door of Shri Ram's Divine Abode and
Hoat na agya binu paisare	without your permission no one can enter Rama's abode.
Sub sukh lahai tumhari sarna	All comforts of the world lie at your feet. The devotees enjoy all
Tum rakshak kahu ko dar na	divine pleasures. You are the protector, why be afraid?
Aapan tej samharo aapei	You alone are befitted to carry your own splendid valour. All the
Teenhon lok hank te kapei	three worlds (entire universe) tremor at your thunderous call.
Bhoot pisach Nikat nahin aavai	All the ghosts, demons and evil forces keep away, with the

Mahavir jab naam sunavai	sheer mention of your great name, O'Mahaveer!!(Hanumanji)
Nase rog harai sab peera	All diseases, pain and suffering disappear on reciting regularly
Japat nirantar Hanumant beera	Shri Hanuman's holy name.
Sankat se Hanuman chudavai	Hanumanji will release those from troubles who meditate upon him in their mind, actions and words.
Man Karam Vachan dyan jo lavai	
Sub par Ram tapasvee raja	Shri Ram as the Supreme Lord and the king of penance.
Tin ke kaj sakal Tum saja	You make all their difficult tasks very easy.
Aur manorath jo koi lavai	Whosoever comes to you for fulfillment of any desire with faith
Sohi amit jeevan phal pavai	and sincerity, they will get imperishable fruit of human life.
Charon Yug partap tumhara	All through the four ages your magnificent glory is acclaimed far
Hai persidh jagat ujiyara	and wide. Your fame is Radiantly acclaimed all over the Cosmos.
Sadhu Sant ke tum Rakhware	You are Saviour and the guardian angel of Saints and Sages and
Asur nikandan Ram dulhare	destroy all Demons. You are the angelic darling of Shri Ram.
Ashta sidhi nav nidhi ke dhata	Mother Sita granted you Eight Siddhis (Eight Supernatural Powers)
Us var deen Janki mata	and Nine divine treasures.

Ram rasayan tumhare pasa	You possess the power of devotion to Shri Ram. In all rebirths
Sada raho Raghupati ke dasa	you will always remain Shri Raghupati's most dedicated disciple.
Tumhare bhajan Ram ko pavai	Through hymns sung in devotion to you, one can find Shri Ram
Janam janam ke dukh bisravai	and become free from sufferings of several births.
Anth kaal Raghuvir pur jayee	If at the time of death one enters the Divine Abode of Shri Ram,
Jahan janam Hari-Bakht Kahayee	thereafter in all future births he is born as the Lord's devotee.
Aur Devta Chit na dharehi	Not contemplating on other deity, as devotion of Shri Hanumanji
Hanumanth se hi sarve sukh karehi	alone can give all happiness.
Sankat kate mite sab peera	Pains and all afflictions will have no place in the life of
Jo sumirai Hanumat Balbeera	one who adores and remember Shri Hanumanji.
Jai Jai Jai Hanuman Gosahin	Let your victory over the evil be firm and final.
Kripa Karahu Gurudev ki nyahin	Bless me and show mercy in the capacity as my supreme guru (teacher).
Jo sat bar path kare kohi	One who recites Chalisa one hundred times, becomes free from the
Chutehi bandhi maha sukh hohi	bondage of life and death and enjoys the highest bliss at last.

Jo yah padhe Hanuman Chalisa	All those who recite Hanuman Chalisa (The forty Chaupais-verses)
Hoye siddhi sakhi Gaureesa	regularly are sure to be benedicted. Lord Shiwa is the witness To this statement.
Tulsidas sada hari chera	Tulsidas is always a disciple of Lord Rama, stays perpetually at
Keejai Das Hrdaye mein dera	his feet, he prays "Oh Lord! You enshrine within my heart & soul."

|| DOHA ||

Pavantnai sankar haran,	Oh! conqueror of the Wind, remover of all difficulties, you are a
Mangal murti roop.	symbol of Auspiciousness.
Ram Lakhan Sita sahit,	Along with Shri Ram, Lakshman and Sita, reside in ourheart.
Hrdaye basahu sur bhoop.	Oh! King of Gods.

Printed in the United States
By Bookmasters